THE BBC TV SHAKESPEARE
Literary Consultant: John Wilders

# ROMEO AND JULIET

THE BBC TV SHAKESPEARE

AS YOU LIKE IT
HENRY VIII
JULIUS CAESAR
MEASURE FOR MEASURE
RICHARD II
ROMEO AND JULIET

THE BBC TV SHAKESPEARE

Literary Consultant: John Wilders
Fellow of Worcester College, Oxford

# Romeo and Juliet

MAYFLOWER BOOKS, INC.,
575 LEXINGTON AVENUE,
NEW YORK CITY 10022.

Published in the United States by Mayflower Books Inc., New York City 10022.

Originally published in England by The British Broadcasting Corporation, 35 Marylebone High Street, London W1M 4AA, England.

The text of *Romeo and Juliet* used in this volume is the Alexander text, edited by the late Professor Peter Alexander and chosen by the BBC as the basis for its television production, and is reprinted by arrangement with William Collins Sons and Company Ltd. The complete Alexander text is published in one volume by William Collins Sons and Company Ltd under the title *The Alexander Text of the Complete Works of William Shakespeare*.



**Library of Congress Cataloging in Publication Data**

Shakespeare, William, 1564–1616.
Romeo and Juliet.

(His The BBC Shakespeare)
I. Wilders, John. II. Title. III. Series: Shakespeare, William, 1564–1616. Selected works. 1978–
PR2831.A23 1978 822.3'3 78–24129

ISBN 0–8317–7469–X

Manufactured in England

First American Edition

CONTENTS

# PREFACE

## Cedric Messina

Is *Romeo and Juliet* the most popular of all Shakespeare's plays? Along with *Julius Caesar* it appears in nearly every school curriculum in the English-speaking world. It has been televised, filmed, made into operas and ballets, symphonically overtured, and turned into a Broadway musical, *West Side Story*, with music by Leonard Bernstein. It has been televised by the BBC five or six times across the years, but this is its first production in colour.

The plays of William Shakespeare have been performed not only in theatres, but also in country houses, inns and courtyards, and one of the earliest references to performances was made by William Keeting, a Naval Commander who kept a journal of a voyage to the East Indies in 1607. The entry for 5 September, off the coast of Sierra Leone, refers to a performance of *Hamlet*, and that of 30 September to a performance of *Richard II*, both being staged for Portuguese visitors aboard the East India Company's ship *Dragon*. And so the plays started their triumphant progress of performances throughout the civilised world.

BBC Television is not inexperienced in the presentation of Shakespeare's plays, and indeed as early as 1937, on the first regular television service in the world, it presented a full-length version of *Julius Caesar*. Since then, thirty of the plays have been presented, the more popular ones many times over. Some have been produced in encapsulated form like *An Age of Kings*; some done on location like *Hamlet* at Elsinore with Christopher Plummer as the Prince and Robert Shaw as Claudius, and *Twelfth Night* at Castle Howard in Yorkshire with Janet Suzman leading the cast as Viola. Studio productions have included *The Tragedy of King Lear,* and *The Merchant of Venice* with Maggie Smith as a memorable Portia. Many productions have been taken from the theatre and translated into television terms like the Royal Shakespeare Company's *The Wars of the Roses* and The National Theatre Zeffirelli production of *Much Ado About Nothing*.

In the discharging of its many duties as a Public Broadcasting Service the BBC has presented during the last ten years at peak viewing time on BBC 1, on every fourth Sunday night, *Play of the Month*, a series of classical productions ranging from all the major plays of Chekhov to a number of Shavian masterpieces. Aeschylus has been produced in the series, and so have many of the plays of William Shakespeare. So not only in the presentation of Shakespeare, but also in the translation to the screen of the great dramatic statements of all ages and countries has the BBC demonstrated that it is fully equipped to meet the enormous challenge of *The BBC Television Shakespeare*.

The autumn of 1975 gave birth to the idea of recording the complete canon of the thirty-seven plays of the national playwright. (Thirty-six of the plays were published in the First Folio of 1623, exactly half of which had never been published before. The thirty-seventh is *Pericles, Prince of Tyre,* first published in the Quarto of 1609.) The first memo on the subject of televising all the plays emanated from my office on 3 November 1975 and was addressed to Alasdair Milne, then Director of Programmes, and now Managing Director, Television. We were asking for his blessing on the project. His reply was immediate and enthusiastic, as was that of the present Director-General, Ian Trethowan. This warm response to the idea stimulated us in the Plays Department to explore the possibility of making the plan a reality – six plays per year for six years, with one odd man out. It has been called the greatest project the BBC has ever undertaken.

There followed a succession of meetings, conferences, discussions and logistical quotations from engineers, designers, costume designers, make-up artists, financial advisers, educational authorities, university dons and musicians. The Literary Consultant, Dr John Wilders, was appointed, as was David Lloyd-Jones as Music Adviser. Alan Shallcross was made responsible for the preparation of the texts. On the island of Ischia, off the coast of Italy, Sir William Walton composed the opening fanfare for the title music for the series. Visits were made to the United States of America to finalise coproduction deals, decisions were taken about the length of the presentations to average about two and a half hours per play, and more seriously, the order of their transmission. This was a game played by many interested parties, some suggesting the plays be presented chronologically, which would have meant the series opening with the comparatively unknown *Henry VI Parts 1, 2 and 3*. This idea was hastily abandoned. A judicious mixture of comedy, tragedy and history seemed the best answer to the problem. It was decided that the English histories, from *Richard II* through all the *Henry IVs, V* and *VIs* to *Richard III* would be presented in chronological order, so that some day in the not too distant future, the eight plays that form this sequence will be able to be seen in their historical order, a unique record of the chronicled history of that time. The plays that form the first sequence will be *Romeo and Juliet, Richard II, As You Like It, Julius Caesar, Measure for Measure* and *Henry VIII*.

The guiding principle behind *The BBC Television Shakespeare* is to make the plays, in permanent form, accessible to audiences throughout the world, and to bring to these many millions the sheer delight and excitement of seeing them in performance – in many cases, for the first time. For students, these productions will offer a wonderful opportunity to study the plays performed by some of the greatest classical actors of our time. But it is a primary intention that the plays are offered as entertainment, to be made as vividly alive as it is possible for the production teams to make them. They are not intended to be museum-like examples of past productions. It is this new commitment, for six plays of Shakespeare per year for six years, that makes the project unique.

In the thirty-seven plays there are a thousand speaking parts, and they demand the most experienced of actors and the most excellent of directors to bring them to life. In the field of directors we are very fortunate, for many of the brilliant practitioners in this series of plays have had wide experience in the classics, both on television and in the theatre. The directors are responsible for the interpretations we shall see, but as the series progresses it will be fascinating to see how many of the actors take these magnificent parts and make them their own.

It was decided to publish the plays, using the Peter Alexander edition, the same text as used in the production of the plays, and one very widely used in the academic world. But these texts with their theatrical divisions into scenes and acts are supplemented with their television equivalents. In other words we are also publishing the television scripts on which the production was based. There are colour and black and white photographs of the production, a general introduction to the play by Dr John Wilders and an article by Henry Fenwick which includes interviews with the actors, directors, designers and costume designers, giving their reactions to the special problems their contributions encountered in the transfer of the plays to the screen. The volumes include a newly compiled glossary and a complete cast list of the performers, including the names of the technicians, costume designers and scenic designers responsible for the play.

The First Quarto version of *Romeo and Juliet* was printed in 1597 entitled

*AN EXCELLENT*
*conceited tragedie*
*OF*
*ROMEO and JULIET*
*As it hath been often (with great applause)*
*plaid publiquely, by the right HONOURABLE*
*the L. of Hunsdon*
*his Servants*

This Quarto has always been considered one of the 'bad' Quartos, being full of inaccuracies, with many speeches abridged. The Second Quarto of 1599 contained 700 more lines than the First. This was followed by three others, the last being printed in 1637. It was the Third Quarto which served as the copy for *Romeo and Juliet*'s inclusion in the First Folio of 1623. The play has 3050 lines, of which 480 have been cut, as is shown in the accompanying text. The major cut has been in the speech Friar Lawrence makes in the last Act, in which he recapitulates, at great length, the story which the audience has just seen enacted before their very eyes. *Romeo and Juliet* is tenth in the accepted chronological order of the plays. This production was recorded on videotape at the BBC Television Centre, White City, London, in February 1978.

There are three magnificent parts for young actors to play: Romeo, Juliet and Mercutio. Old Capulet and the Nurse are equally telling. Casting the role of Juliet has always been a great problem. She requires three attributes seldom found in one performer. She should be thirteen years old, have great acting skill, and the emotional depth in her portrayal to play a girl in love, a bride, and, for a few moments, a widow. One or two of these demands are often met in performance, but it is the first demand – the age – that is so often difficult to meet. In this production, after many, many auditions of many, many aspirants, the role was entrusted to a fourteen-year-old London grammar school girl, Rebecca Saire. How many of these demands are met in her performance you will be able to determine as this great lyrical tragedy unfolds.

# INTRODUCTION TO ROMEO AND JULIET

John Wilders

*Romeo and Juliet* contains one of the best-known lines in the literature of the world, the words spoken by Juliet as she stands on her balcony, unaware of Romeo concealed in the darkness of the orchard below:

> O Romeo, Romeo! Wherefore art thou Romeo?

The line has become celebrated not by accident but because Shakespeare used all the resources of his art to ensure that it would make a deep impression on his audience. To try and discover why it creates such an effect is to learn something about Shakespeare's skill as a dramatist and about the tragedy itself.

The power of the line is produced partly by the care with which Shakespeare has placed it in relation to what has gone before, and partly by the implications of the few, simple words themselves, which have a significance for Juliet's predicament, for the play generally and for the human condition as Shakespeare portrays it.

Shakespeare has been preparing the audience for this moment from the very start of the tragedy and, when it occurs, it breaks upon us both as a climax and a summary of the action. By this point in the play we are well aware of the long-continued feud between the Montagues and the Capulets and have seen it burst into open violence; we have felt the danger in which Romeo has placed himself by going disguised to the Capulets' ball; we have watched the first encounter between Romeo and Juliet and their instantaneous passion for each other, an adoration they can express only guardedly, because neither knows how the other will respond, and furtively in the threatening presence of his enemies and her family. When, therefore, the two are at last alone in the orchard, we are gratified for their sakes and attentive to their words. The balcony scene, moreover, stands out in contrast to the two scenes which have preceded it, the brightly-lit, animated, crowded scene at the ball (I v) and the rowdy, high-spirited street scene (II i) in which Benvolio and Mercutio shout obscenities at the hidden Romeo. The change of focus from the street to the orchard is from noise to stillness, bawdy jokes to romantic love, the open streets to the enclosed garden where the darkness is illuminated by the single light from Juliet's balcony towards which Romeo gazes. Moreover, though the lovers are now alone, Juliet is unaware of Romeo's presence and the suspense is heightened because, for a while, she says nothing; her first sound is an expressive 'Ay me!' It is at this carefully prepared moment, as though in reply to Romeo's unheard plea, 'O, speak again, bright angel', that she delivers the lines which Shakespeare's art has made memorable:

O Romeo, Romeo! wherefore art thou Romeo?
Deny thy father and refuse thy name;
Or, if thou wilt not, be but sworn my love,
And I'll no longer be a Capulet.

*Romeo and Juliet*, whatever else we may think of it, is obviously the work of a man who knows how to sustain and control the responses of an audience.

Juliet's actual words have a significance for the rest of the tragedy. Her first line is a question about names, and names have a

*The Ball. Rebecca Saire as Juliet and Christopher Northey as Paris*

particular importance in this play. For example, when Juliet has first met Romeo at the ball, she sends the nurse with the instruction, 'Go ask his name'. Again, when the newly-married Romeo encounters Tybalt, he addresses him as

> Good Capulet – which name I tender
> As dearly as mine own.

And Romeo's sense of his own name is expressed most violently when, after he has killed Tybalt and lies concealed in the Friar's cell, he treats it as though it had an independent existence:

> That name's cursed hand
> Murder'd her kinsman. O, tell me, friar, tell me,
> In what vile part of this anatomy
> Doth my name lodge? Tell me that I may sack
> The hateful mansion.

His impulse is to destroy himself and thereby to eradicate his own guilty name.

Each of the lovers has a family name, Montague and Capulet, and these represent the unbreakable chains which bind them to their respective, warring households; it represents the enmity into which they have been born. And each has a unique name, Romeo and Juliet, which signifies his individuality, those qualities which distinguish and separate each of them from all the other Montagues and Capulets. 'Romeo' signifies the particular 'face, leg, hand, foot and body' to which the nurse refers admiringly and with which Juliet has fallen in love. One way of understanding the play is to see it as the attempt and the tragic failure of the two young people to 'deny their names' and thereby to become exclusively themselves. They are, needless to say, attempting the impossible.

Juliet's 'Wherefore?' (or 'For what cause?') is one of the lovers' many uncomprehending protests against a hidden and malevolent power in the heavens which has decreed that the one person most dear to them should have been born into that family which most hates their own: 'My only love sprung from my only hate!', as Juliet succinctly declares. It is against these same powers that Romeo cries out in the most bitterly searching lines of the play:

> Heaven is here
> Where Juliet lives, and every cat and dog,
> And little mouse, every unworthy thing,
> Live here in heaven, and may look on her;
> But Romeo may not.

This is an anguished complaint against the injustice of the supernatural powers which seem to govern the world. Shakespeare, incidentally, was to recall and revise these words of Romeo's in the most tragically bleak moment in his entire works, the moment when King Lear stands, holding in his arms the body of his dearest child:

> No, no, no life!
> Why should a dog, a horse, a rat have life,
> And thou no breath at all?

As well as being, at this relatively early stage in his career, a brilliantly skilled writer for the theatre, Shakespeare was also able to look beyond the immediate, specific predicament of his characters to the greater metaphysical powers which seem to have placed them in it.

Shakespeare shows us very vividly what it means to be a Capulet and a Montague. His quick, lively sketches of the domestic life of the Capulets are among the small triumphs of *Romeo and Juliet*. The family belongs to the wealthy Italian upper middle class which he had already portrayed in *The Taming of the Shrew*, written about a year earlier. It is dominated by the father, a fussy, impatient, easily flustered little dictator, generously hospitable to his guests, but determined to impose his will over the younger generation, such as Tybalt (when the latter struggles to attack Romeo during the ball), and particularly Juliet when she defiantly refuses to marry Paris. Shakespeare rapidly sketches into the background of the play the agitation and concern for material comfort in the Capulet family by inserting a short dialogue between the servants at the opening of the scene at the ball:

> Away with the join-stools, remove the court-cubbert, look to the plate. Good thou, save me a piece of marchpane; and as thou loves me let the porter let in Susan Grindstone and Nell. Antony, and Potpan!

We can size up the Capulets on the evidence of these two hurriedly spoken sentences: the sense of confusion (also conveyed by Capulet himself during the ball) suggests that they do not put on their social entertainments with quite the ease and confidence of the aristocracy, yet they are wealthy enough to possess silver plate, to serve marchpane (marzipan) to their guests, and to employ a number of servants. (Since they have to be 'let in', Susan, Nell, Antony and Potpan may be extra, hired help.) A similar impression is created as the family prepare through the night for the wedding reception with such haste that Juliet's parents themselves appear to be giving a hand with the cooking:

*Lady Capulet.* Hold, take these keys, and fetch more spices, nurse.
*Nurse.* They call for dates and quinces in the pastry.
*Capulet.* Come, stir, stir, stir! The second cock hath crow'd,
The curfew bell hath rung, 'tis three o'clock.
Look to the bak'd meats, good Angelica;
Spare not for cost.

It is consistent with what we know of her family background that, during her first scene (I iii), Juliet is shown to be a thoroughly conventional, polite, submissive daughter. She is, after all, only thirteen, and when she first appears she remains almost totally silent for nearly seventy lines. On being asked whether she is inclined to marriage, she modestly replies,

It is an honour that I dream not of,

and she agrees to love only a man whom her parents have chosen for her. It is easy to imagine what Juliet might have become: married to a Count, comfortably well off, producing grandchildren for her parents to dote over, and remaining passive and conventional for the rest of her life. Her love for Romeo transforms her life and personality: she acquires an independence of mind, sleeps in secret with her husband under her parents' roof, defies her father's wrath, and resolutely kills herself when Romeo is dead. She ceases to be a Capulet and becomes Juliet. Yet by the process of coming to life she ensures her early death. 'So quick bright things come to confusion.'

Shakespeare shows us very little of Romeo's parents, and their relative absence is deliberate, for we see a great deal of his companions: he is at the age when young men stay out late and roam the streets in gangs. Shakespeare has identified a difference between the young Italian male and female which can still be seen today. Benvolio and Mercutio are boisterous, earthy, daring, irresponsible youths, affectionate towards one another but contemptuous of their sworn enemies, the Capulets. In their own way they are as conventional as Juliet's parents. Romeo has already, early in the play, begun to move away from the group as a result of his infatuation with his first love, Rosaline, but his passion for Juliet divorces him completely from them. This separation is shown visually in the scene (II i) where, as his friends call out for him in the street, he hides from them behind the Capulets' wall. Again when, after his marriage, he is challenged by Tybalt, he replies most unconventionally:

> I do protest I never injur'd thee,
> But love thee better than thou canst devise
> Till thou shalt know the reason of my love;
> And so, good Capulet – which name I tender
> As dearly as mine own – be satisfied.

– a response which Mercutio treats with shocked contempt. In acquiring a wife, Romeo has lost the qualities which marked him as a Montague, a member of the gang; Juliet's beauty, as he puts it, has made him effeminate and he tries, disastrously, to stop the quarrel. His love, like hers, raises him above convention and yet contributes to his – and Mercutio's – death. Their love makes the hero and heroine fully themselves and also ruins them. By a similar paradox, each commits suicide as the supreme expression of love for the other. Their end is a death in love and a love in death.

The Montagues and the Capulets resemble each other, however, in the extreme intensity of their emotions. The first image Shakespeare gives us is of the violent enmity between the two families, a smouldering animosity which, within seconds, flares up into physical violence, sparked off by Tybalt's ferocious challenge:

> What, drawn, and talk of peace! I hate the word,
> As I hate hell, all Montagues, and thee.

Capulet is constantly in a state of fevered agitation which turns to rage when his will is crossed by Tybalt or Juliet. Moreover, the families are as unrestrained in sorrow as they are in hatred: Romeo's reaction to the news of his banishment is to collapse on the floor, 'blubbering and weeping, weeping and blubbering', and, on the apparent death of their daughter, the Capulets pour out their grief in a great torrent of complaint and lamentation. So violent are their passions that some of the characters shake, physically, under their pressure: Tybalt's 'flesh trembles' with rage, and the nurse, taunted by the young Montagues, becomes so vexed that 'every part' about her 'quivers'. The overwhelming love which Romeo and Juliet experience is, therefore, consistent with the high emotions which possess almost everyone. Only the Friar remains calm, cautious and fearful of its consequences:

These violent delights have violent ends,
And in their triumph die; like fire and powder,
Which, as they kiss, consume.

The impression of lives lived intensely is also created by the high speed at which the action moves. No sooner do the servants meet than they fight; no sooner have the lovers glimpsed each other than they become infatuated; no sooner does Romeo hear of Juliet's death than he resolves on suicide, demanding a poison that will work

As violently as hasty powder fir'd
Doth hurry from the fatal cannon's womb.

As soon as she sees her husband's body, Juliet unhesitatingly kills herself. The action of the play, as Shakespeare takes care to inform us, occupies only four days. The opening brawl takes place on a Sunday morning, the lovers meet that night, are married on the Monday afternoon, and rise from their night together the following morning. On that same Tuesday, Juliet drinks the potion and is discovered by the nurse early on Wednesday. By dawn on the Thursday, both are dead. The tragedy seems to be driven forward by the emotional ferocity of the characters.

Shakespeare interrupts the headlong rush of the action, however, with interludes where time seems to be suspended. They occur, as we might expect, when Romeo and Juliet are alone, and the motionless tranquillity of their meetings is one of the qualities which isolates them from everyone else. They attempt to make for themselves a private world, cut off from the time-bound activities of ancient feuds and hasty matchmaking. They struggle in vain towards the kind of love celebrated in the poetry of Donne (which was written at about the same time as this play, 1595), a love where 'nothing else is', one which

no tomorrow hath, nor yesterday,
Running it never runs from us away,
But truly keeps his first, last, everlasting day.

Circumstances make such an achievement impossible. They are alone together only three times: in the Capulets' orchard, in Juliet's bedroom and in the tomb, a hasty, secretive courtship, marriage and death which make their tragedy the more pitiful. The apparent immunity of their world is suggested by the fact that they meet only at night and in enclosed spaces. This is partly for practical reasons – they fear to be discovered – but it also creates the impression of an intimate, night-time world where they alone are fully awake. The darkness is illuminated for them by their own brightness. Each refers to the other as a light: to Romeo, Juliet's window is 'the east' and she 'the sun'; to Juliet, Romeo should be 'cut out in little stars' which would make all the world 'in love with night'. Shakespeare makes good dramatic use of Juliet's balcony, a secret, magical place which can be reached only with difficulty and danger: the physical height of the balcony raises them metaphorically above the rest of the world, an idea which Romeo expresses as he stands in the orchard, gazing upwards at Juliet:

> O, speak again, bright angel, for thou art
> As glorious to this night, being o'er my head,
> As is a winged messenger of heaven
> Unto the white-upturned wond'ring eyes
> Of mortals that fall back to gaze on him,
> When he bestrides the lazy-pacing clouds
> And sails upon the bosom of the air.

Their privacy is, however, always at risk and always invaded by an alien world: their courtship is interrupted by the impatient call of the nurse, and their wedding night by the fateful song of the lark which summons Romeo to his banishment.

Each of the lovers has a close companion and confidant who seems to be helpful to them but, in the event, proves fatal. Mercutio and the nurse are the most fully and distinctively characterised people in the play. The former, like Romeo, is only partially engaged in the family feud, which he regards with a half-mocking detachment, yet, like Romeo, he becomes a victim of it. In the 'Queen Mab' speech, a kind of aria without music, Shakespeare reveals the man's witty intelligence (in contrast to Romeo's romantic passion), his sociability as an entertainer and his worldly sophistication. At the same time he establishes him as a substantial, engaging figure in order that his death may create a serious sense of loss. The nurse is the most recognisably human of all the characters: as soon as she embarks on her first, rambling, affectionate, earthy reminiscences of Juliet as a baby, she stands solidly real. Like many women of easy morals she is sentimental and is sufficiently detached from the war of the families, acting as a go-between for the lovers, that we trust her as a dependable ally. The moment when she casually reveals that she is not comes, therefore, as a brutal shock:

Then, since the case so stands as now it doth,
I think it best you married with the County.
O, he's a lovely gentleman!
Romeo's a dishclout to him.

Not only is she advising bigamy to a newly-married, thirteen-year-old girl, but she shows a blindness towards Juliet's kind of love which leaves the heroine completely isolated. Thus deprived, through Mercutio's death, Romeo's banishment and the nurse's betrayal, of their only allies, the lovers are left to meet their deaths in pitiful isolation.

Shakespeare seems to have thought of *Romeo and Juliet* as a tragedy of fate, brought about by supernatural forces which the lovers are too weak to resist. They are 'star-crossed' lovers, whose 'ill-divining souls' dimly foresee 'some bitter consequence yet hanging in the stars' which will destroy them. Romeo's impulse on hearing of Juliet's death is to taunt the heavens who have contrived it:

Is it e'en so? Then, I defy you, stars.

And he welcomes his own suicide as a positive act which will

shake the yoke of inauspicious stars
From this world-wearied flesh.

In fact, the tragedy results from a variety of causes: the rash, impulsive actions of nearly all the protagonists, the sheer bad luck which delays Friar Lawrence's letter and Juliet's awakening from her trance, the miscarriage of the Friar's well-intentioned plans which, in the end, prove fatal. But *Romeo and Juliet* resembles Shakespeare's later tragedies, such as *Othello* and *Hamlet*, in that the catastrophe is brought about, ironically, by the very qualities in the central characters which most commend them to us. The hero and heroine possess that characteristic which A. C. Bradley recognised in Shakespeare's great tragic heroes, 'a fatal tendency to identify the whole being with one interest, object, passion or habit of mind', a tragic quality of character 'which is also his greatness', so that his virtues 'help to destroy him'. Those qualities which distinguish Romeo and Juliet from all the other Montagues and Capulets – their transcendent love, their altruistic courage, the tenderness of their affections, their impulse to be intensely and defiantly themselves – enable them to live more generously for a few hours than others accomplish in a lifetime. Their brief association is both their doom and their triumph.

# THE PRODUCTION

## Henry Fenwick

Alvin Rakoff was working on a television production of Arnold Wesker's *The Kitchen* when he heard that Cedric Messina would like to see him. 'I knew he was doing the Shakespeare project and I knew the likelihood was he was going to offer me one of the Shakespeares. In the car driving to television centre I was wondering which one it would be. I thought: "It's not going to be one of the ones I really like, it's going to be one of the ones I don't understand, like *All's Well*. So when he came out and said it was *Romeo and Juliet* I was delighted. At least I could read it and understand it without too much help."'

Messina and Rakoff had worked together before several times; among other successes they had introduced Lee Remick to British television in Tennessee Williams' *Summer and Smoke*, in a production which won a number of awards, and Messina says he wanted Rakoff for *Romeo* because 'he's very good at romantic stuff – he *is* romantic'. Rakoff, however, although flattered, sees himself as just as much of an action director. (After *Romeo and Juliet* he went straight on to direct a Henry Fonda action film, *City On Fire*, set in Montreal.) *Romeo and Juliet* has action enough to satisfy him: 'The action sequences help the romance: it's a long play, that play. It's one of his first, it's not the best constructed, it doesn't have his best verse in it, but it's a great play, a great one to do.'

It has always been, and remains, a play of enormous popular appeal, 'because', thinks Messina, 'of the immense drive of the narrative. You must be sitting on the edge of your seat over what's actually going to happen, if you don't know – though I assume everybody in the world knows now. But even when you do know you somehow hope that it won't happen – you still hope Romeo will get on a horse and come hurtling back from Mantua in time.'

It is also a play of immense vitality and, in the early section, humour, as Messina points out: 'With the death of Mercutio, about 1½ hours in, everything begins going radically, hopelessly, terribly wrong. There's not a laugh from there on. But at the beginning even the fight in the first scene is light and easy: when old Capulet calls for his sword his wife mocks him: "A crutch, a crutch! Why call you for a sword?" You think that there's a bit of danger in the market place but you feel it's going to be wafted away with Italian geniality.' It is a play full of suspense, but it is not a doom-ridden play. 'Stop acting as though you know the end,' Rakoff kept telling some of his younger actors.

'How, after so many productions, are you going to mount it in such a way that it will look as though you've never seen it before?' asks Messina, shrugging. After some discussion of dressing the play in the Elizabethan period, the final decision was to 'set it in high Renaissance Tuscany – I don't feel you can do it any other way. It's so encrusted in tradition.' 'It's a very youthful story,' adds costume designer Odette Barrow. 'The Italian Renaissance is a much more youthful period, with the men's tights and tunics. And the women's clothes were very much simpler than the Elizabethan styles, and relied first on fabrics, not so much on overtrimming. I set it in about 1490. For a lot of the research I went to the Witt Library [part of the Courtauld Institute]. I also went to the Mansell Collection – in fact one goes everywhere, the V and A [Victoria and Albert Museum], the libraries. At the Witt they have illustrations of all the artists of the period. You can take photocopies, so provided you can find what you want you can come away with stacks of photocopies and work from there. Having seen all those paintings I was sure 1490 was right – it was so beautiful.' She skims through a bunch of photocopies, showing me sketches by Filippino Lippi, Vittore Carpaccio, Domenico Ghirlandaio, Luca Signorelli to prove her point – which they do, amply. They are extremely beautiful.

Both Rakoff and Messina were sure that the play should be staged as naturalistically as possible. 'You have to see a proper ballroom, a balcony, the garden, the piazza,' Messina insists. 'In order to grab the audience's attention you've got to do it as realistically as possible,' Rakoff stresses. 'You're asking the audience today to do a hell of a thing: the most real medium in the world is television; they're watching the news at nine o'clock and they're seeing real blood and real violence and suddenly we're saying, "Come to our pretend violence." I've done stylised productions before, and it takes the audience a hell of a long time to get with you. You could do *Romeo and Juliet* against white or black drapes but I think you'd alienate a hell of a lot of the potential viewers. I would love to have tried to do *Romeo* outside in a Verona town somewhere.' Both Messina and Rakoff are great admirers of the Zeffirelli productions both on stage and on film. 'In the film version he rightly minimised the dialogue,' says Rakoff, 'and went for those stunning visuals – which you can do on film. In a medium which is half-way between theatre and film I was trying to go for the visuals, trying also to go for the words, and trying to erase from my mind Zeffirelli's production – which I think I did. I didn't knowingly pinch anything from him.'

The unique problem *Romeo and Juliet* had in this first season of Shakespeare plays was that of cutting. Experience shows that the maximum length for a television play to hold the viewer's attention is about two and a half hours, says Alan Shallcross, the script editor. 2800 lines of Shakespearian text runs, they discovered, to about two and a quarter hours. *Romeo and Juliet*, of the six plays in the first season, was the only one with over 3000 lines. Cutting, therefore, which had not been a major matter on the other productions, became an important issue. Obviously the problem is going to be one of growing importance in the coming years, when the longer plays are televised, and a decision has already been taken in principle to run 'the biggies' (*Hamlet*, *Lear*, etc.) in extenso, probably across two nights. But with *Romeo and Juliet* it seemed possible to pare down to two and a half hours without losing the natural shape of the play. Discussions on cuts took place between director, script editor, and literary consultant John Wilders, deciding what should go because it was no longer comprehensible to a modern audience, what was extraneous because it was unnecessary repetition, employed by Shakespeare for stagecraft reasons, to make sure that a distracted and noisy audience picked up crucial points of plot. Basically cuts were taken in rehearsal, says Rakoff. 'Sometimes an actor would say, "I don't understand this line, I can't make it make sense." I think Shakespeare would have understood and said, "Cut it". He was a professional actor too. Sometimes I would bully the actors into doing things they wanted to leave out because I needed the moment. One is torn. Cedric's brief was to make it as definitive as you can. To do a definitive version you have to do the whole text really. One didn't want to cut too much, but as a showman you don't want to bore the pants off your audience, so some sort of compromise has to be made. But whoever does Shakespeare, it will always be true – certain things you cannot make sense of and they should be cut.'

The major change, says Shallcross, came at the end. The Prince, the warring families and the citizens of Verona gather to view the bodies of the lovers, and Friar Lawrence, the holy man whose plans have gone awry, recounts the whole story we have already seen enacted, for the benefit of the characters on stage who aren't as informed as the audience. Instead of listening to the whole tale recounted again 'with great tedium', says Shallcross, 'we try to tell the story as Shakespeare would have done as a television practitioner.' Therefore not only is a large part of Friar Lawrence's speech deleted but, using the camera's ability to cut from place to place, certain parts of the final scene are rearranged to help the telling of the story.

When casting the play there were two cast choices which were unexpected, possibly controversial. The first was the casting of Rebecca Saire as Juliet. Rebecca was a girl of only fourteen at the time – the right age for Juliet but obviously without the technical equipment or experience often felt necessary for the part. Rakoff and his assistant saw over 300 actresses and finally narrowed the possibilities down to three: Rebecca, and an actress of eighteen, and one of twenty-five. 'They were *very* talented but television is a very hard medium – there's that close-up and there's no way in which you can make a 25-year-old actress look fourteen. I called Rebecca back about three or four times and eventually I saw her with both Cedric and Jimmy [Cellan-Jones, head of BBC Television Drama Plays] and they both said the girl was a natural. She does have limitations – which you're bound to have at that age – but at least she is fourteen. She looks like a young child killing herself.'

'We have a daughter of seven and a half,' says Messina, 'and I could see her in Rebecca. Juliet is a child. Of course the sort of words Shakespeare gives her are not a child's words – it's not written like that. But then you find yourself in terrible, terrible trouble about ages in *Romeo*: what, for example, is the age of the nurse? She's supposed to have been Juliet's wet nurse and has always been played by an old character actress, whereas she was suckling Juliet thirteen years before. There's the age of Juliet's mother: she says to Juliet, 'I was your mother much upon these years That you are now a maid,' which makes her about twenty-six to twenty-eight. But at another moment she talks of going to her grave. Once you start these arithmetical age countings you go out of your mind with Shakespeare.'

'It's simple to explain,' says Rakoff. 'Shakespeare didn't have a continuity girl. If it felt right he said it, and nobody said to him:

“Oh, by the way, you can’t say that because earlier . . .” After all, how old would a 28-year-old woman at that time look? How old would a wet nurse look fourteen years after her teats were drying? At forty women were dying in those days, and they were outliving the men. Thirty-eight was old. But mainly, whatever Mr Shakespeare wanted to say at the moment, he said. This is why you see all the professors going through hoops trying to make it make sense. But there’s no way you can.’

The other casting surprise was that of Celia Johnson as the nurse, a part far from her more usual image of genteel English lady. ‘The nurse is usually cast for great raucous comedy relief,’ says Rakoff. ‘But the nurse is going to be comedy relief no matter what you do with it. I loved the way Celia did it, marvellous and televisual and the right degree of comedy. I think she is a great actress. The more I thought of it the more I found everybody else seemed very obvious. I rang her and said, “Can you get far enough down the social scale?” and she said, “Sure I could,” and I said, “That’s all I was worried about.” ’

I remark to him that the strong performance of Celia Johnson, combined with the extreme youth of Rebecca Saire, make an unusually intense unit of Juliet and the nurse together. ‘Until the time that Juliet breaks out,’ he says, ‘there should be a strong feeling of a household. The first words of the play, spoken by Sir John Gielgud [Chorus], are “Two households”. It’s very important to realise that the Capulet family is a happy family, should have gone on being an absolutely happy family. Had Juliet not met this interloper called Montague she would have married Paris and they would have had – not a great marriage but it would have worked – it would have been an ordinary suburban marriage as we all know it and it would have been perfectly acceptable and she would have been perfectly happy. I think Shakespeare believes in family unity and it was essential that Michael Hordern [Capulet] and Jacqueline Hill [Lady Capulet] and the child and the nurse be a unit – a unit destroyed by circumstances. If the family unit is tight it heightens the tragedy. I’ve never seen the family unit quite so close-knit as I make it and I do think that’s the most important contribution I bring to this production.’

Rakoff also stresses the fact that this is a bourgeois family: ‘It’s one of the few Shakespeare plays where he’s not dealing with nobility. They’re very rich and I think some of the things he has them do are very bourgeois. Even at the end, when old Montague says, “I will raise her statue in pure gold,” Capulet says: “As rich shall Romeo's by his lady's lie." How bourgeois can you get? My swimming pool's going to be bigger than your swimming pool and my car is going to be bigger than your car. I know it's meant on a much more romantic level but that element is there. They were very wealthy families, both of them, but very bourgeois.

'Once we were sure of that it helped me in the staging. With Shakespeare the usual thing is you come on and say your lines, but making them bourgeois I could make Michael Hordern go shopping with his servant Peter. I could make the scene after Tybalt's death, when Paris comes to woo Juliet and she won't come down from her room, into a dinner scene with servants standing around and everybody finishing eating. The actors rebelled, consciously or unconsciously, at first: Michael used to call the shopping scene the Sainsbury scene. This was an indication of how the actors regarded it. Michael Hordern had done much more Shakespeare than I have and suddenly I was saying, "I don't want you just coming on screen and saying your lines; I want you to say them while you're smelling fish, buying melons."'

Messina is delighted with the result. 'To me one of the most astounding performances is Michael Hordern's. I've never seen Capulet played like that. He's just an old drunk who loves a good party; he wants to have a good time all the time; he gets drunk at the party, falls about, gets carried upstairs – then suddenly this awful tragedy occurs. But up to that moment in time he's just an old lush having a good time around Verona, going to and giving as many parties as he possibly can. The first time I saw *Romeo and Juliet* was a very long time ago – an old Metro-Goldwyn-Mayer movie with Norma Shearer and Leslie Howard and Basil Rathbone. John Barrymore was Mercutio. The average age of the four of them was round about forty-five. Sir C. Aubrey Smith, who was a great 6′ 2″ English character actor in Hollywood films from the thirties onwards, played Capulet as this grand old English cricketing gentleman. When old Michael runs around buying the vegetables, getting the drink in, jollying the servants along, being irritable – I think it's a great eye-opener of a performance.'

Rakoff also brought a startling new slant to the Romeo–Tybalt fight, where the play starts its slide into catastrophe. It is a killing of startling brutality. Fight director William Hobbs had staged the *Romeo* fights in previous productions about twenty-five times, but still felt that the way he and the director staged them this time around had never been done before in his experience. 'Mercutio is not afraid of Tybalt,' says Rakoff. 'I took Mercutio's lines objectively; when he threatens Tybalt and says, "Here's that shall make you dance", he's not afraid of him. He'd rather not fight him: two good fighters would rather not fight in any situation – they respect each other too much. But Mercutio is not afraid of Tybalt – Tybalt is the Jack Palance character in the cowboy movie, he can outdraw anybody, but Mercutio thinks he's as good. He just doesn't go around expressing it. Their fight could be both classic, tiring and funny – Mercutio is a funny character and he would fight funny. David agreed on that.

'The two fights follow each other and what I wanted for Romeo and Tybalt was a bloody great brawl by comparison. It has to be sordid, as sordid as possible. In fact, if I'd had more time I would have done a few extra things that would have made it even more sordid. The Mercutio–Tybalt fight is a classic fight, a good fight. The other one is a street brawl. Romeo can't fight Tybalt. The only reason he wins in my mind is that Tybalt is tired and Romeo's so furious that his passion kills Tybalt. In a straight duel he'd never have beaten him. Tybalt was better than Mercutio and Mercutio was better than Romeo. It's just that Romeo is incensed, passionate: he's very young and can't control his emotions, and it's a sordid fight: Romeo kicks Tybalt in the balls, puts the sword in, and continues plunging with the knife – it's not even a clean rapier wound, it's a dagger, plunged in again and again and again.'

The sequence is proof of Rakoff's claim to be an action director. But the sequence of which he seems proudest is the ball at which Romeo and Juliet meet. Technically it was the highlight of the shooting for him. 'We did the dance in one take,' he says proudly. 'Fifteen minutes in one take. We did our lighting and got to it right after lunch. From the moment the yobs – the boys – the teenagers make their entrance until the end of the dance, just before Sir John's second entrance as the chorus, that's all one take. Towards the end I began to think: fourteen minutes and nothing's gone wrong! *I'd* better not blow it! Geraldine Stephenson had choreographed it and it was a great camera crew. Jim Atkinson, who's about to retire, was in charge, everybody was working at their best, knowing it was possible. Television precision!'

# THE BBC TV CAST AND PRODUCTION TEAM

The cast for the BBC television production was as follows:

| | |
|---|---|
| Romeo | Patrick Ryecart |
| Juliet | Rebecca Saire |
| Nurse | Celia Johnson |
| Capulet | Michael Hordern |
| Chorus | John Gielgud |
| Friar | Joseph O'Conor |
| Prince Escalus | Laurence Naismith |
| Mercutio | Anthony Andrews |
| Tybalt | Alan Rickman |
| Lady Capulet | Jacqueline Hill |
| Benvolio | Christopher Strauli |
| Paris | Christopher Northey |
| Peter | Paul Henry |
| Balthasar | Roger Davidson |
| Montague | John Paul |
| Lady Montague | Zulema Dene |
| Old Capulet | Esmond Knight |
| Sampson | David Sibley |
| Gregory | Jack Carr |
| Abraham | Bunny Reed |
| Apothecary | Vernon Dobtcheff |
| Friar John | John Savident |
| Musician | Danny Schiller |
| First Watch | Jeremy Young |
| Second Watch | Jeffrey Chiswick |
| Potpan | Gary Taylor |
| Pages | Mark Arden |
| | Robert Burbage |
| First Citizen | Alan Bowerman |
| Choreographer | Geraldine Stephenson |

| | |
|---|---|
| FIGHT DIRECTOR | William Hobbs |
| PRODUCTION ASSISTANT | Carol Robertson |
| PRODUCTION UNIT MANAGER | Fraser Lowden |
| MUSIC | James Tyler and the London Early Music Group |
| MUSIC ADVISER | David Lloyd-Jones |
| LITERARY CONSULTANT | John Wilders |
| MAKE-UP ARTIST | Dawn Alcock |
| COSTUME DESIGNER | Odette Barrow |
| SOUND | Colin Dixon |
| LIGHTING | John Treays |
| DESIGNER | Stuart Walker |
| SCRIPT EDITOR | Alan Shallcross |
| PRODUCER | Cedric Messina |
| DIRECTOR | Alvin Rakoff |

The production was recorded between 31 January and 5 February 1978

# THE TEXT

In order to help readers who might wish to use this text to follow the play on the screen the scene divisions and locations used in the television production and any cuts and rearrangements made are shown in the right-hand margins. The principles governing these annotations are as follows:

1. Where a new location (change of set) is used by the TV production this is shown as a new scene. The scenes are numbered consecutively, and each one is identified as exterior or interior, located by a brief description of the set or the location, and placed in its 'time' setting (e.g. Day, Night, Dawn). These procedures are those used in BBC Television camera scripts.

2. Where the original stage direction shows the entry of a character at the beginning of a scene, this has not been deleted (unless it causes confusion). This is in order to demonstrate which characters are in the scene, since in most cases the TV scene begins with the characters 'discovered' on the set.

3. Where the start of a TV scene does not coincide with the start of a scene in the printed text, the characters in that scene have been listed, *unless* the start of the scene coincides with a stage direction which indicates the entrance of all those characters.

4. Where the text has been cut in the TV production, the cuts are marked by vertical rules and by a note in the margin. If complete lines are cut, these are shown as, e.g., Lines 27–38 omitted. If part of a line only is cut, or in cases of doubt (e.g. in prose passages), the first and last words of the cut are also given.

5. Occasionally, and only when it is thought necessary for comprehension of the action, a note of a character's moves has been inserted in the margin.

6. Where the action moves from one part of a set to another, no attempt has been made to show this as a succession of scenes.

ALAN SHALLCROSS

# ROMEO AND JULIET

## DRAMATIS PERSONÆ

CHORUS.
ESCALUS, *Prince of Verona.*
PARIS, *a young nobleman, kinsman to the Prince.*
MONTAGUE, CAPULET, *heads of two houses at variance with each other.*
AN OLD MAN, *of the Capulet family.*
ROMEO, *son to Montague.*
MERCUTIO, *kinsman to the Prince, and friend to Romeo.*
BENVOLIO, *nephew to Montague, and friend to Romeo.*
TYBALT, *nephew to Lady Capulet.*
FRIAR LAWRENCE, FRIAR JOHN, *Franciscans.*
BALTHASAR, *servant to Romeo.*
SAMPSON, GREGORY, *servants to Capulet.*
PETER, *servant to Juliet's nurse.*
ABRAHAM, *servant to Montague.*
AN APOTHECARY.
THREE MUSICIANS.
AN OFFICER.

LADY MONTAGUE, *wife to Montague.*
LADY CAPULET, *wife to Capulet.*
JULIET, *daughter to Capulet.*
NURSE *to Juliet.*
CITIZENS of VERONA; GENTLEMEN *and* GENTLEWOMEN *of both houses*; MASKERS, TORCH-BEARERS, PAGES, GUARDS, WATCHMEN, SERVANTS, *and* ATTENDANTS.

THE SCENE: *Verona and Mantua.*

## THE PROLOGUE

*Enter* CHORUS.

Two households, both alike in dignity,
In fair Verona, where we lay our scene,
From ancient grudge break to new mutiny,
Where civil blood makes civil hands unclean.
From forth the fatal loins of these two foes
A pair of star-cross'd lovers take their life;
Whose misadventur'd piteous overthrows
Doth with their death bury their parents' strife.
The fearful passage of their death-mark'd love,
And the continuance of their parents' rage,
Which, but their children's end, nought could remove,
Is now the two hours' traffic of our stage;
The which if you with patient ears attend,
What here shall miss, our toil shall strive to mend. [*Exit.*

## ACT ONE

### SCENE I. *Verona. A public place.*

SCENE I
*Exterior. Verona. Day.*

*Enter* SAMPSON *and* GREGORY, *of the house of* CAPULET, *with swords and bucklers on.*

SAM. Gregory, on my word, we'll not carry coals.

GRE. No, for then we should be colliers.

SAM. I mean, an we be in choler, we'll draw.

GRE. Ay, while you live, draw your neck out of collar.

Lines 4–5 omitted.

SAM. I strike quickly, being moved.

GRE. But thou art not quickly moved to strike.

Lines 7–19 omitted.

SAM. A dog of the house of Montague moves me.

GRE. To move is to stir, and to be valiant is to stand; therefore, if thou art moved, thou run'st away.

SAM. A dog of that house shall move me to stand. I will take the wall of any man or maid of Montague's.

GRE. That shows thee a weak slave; for the weakest goes to the wall.

SAM. 'Tis true; and therefore women, being the weaker vessels, are ever thrust to the wall; therefore I will push Montague's men from the wall and thrust his maids to the wall.

GRE. The quarrel is between our masters and us their men.

SAM. 'Tis all one; I will show myself a tyrant. When I have fought with the men, I will be civil with the maids—I will cut off their heads.

GRE. The heads of the maids?

SAM. Ay, the heads of the maids, or their maidenheads; take it in what sense thou wilt.

GRE. They must take it in sense that feel it.

SAM. Me they shall feel while I am able to stand; and 'tis known I am a pretty piece of flesh.

GRE. 'Tis well thou art not fish; if thou hadst, thou hadst been poor-John. Draw thy tool; here comes two of the house of Montagues.

''Tis well . . . poor-John' omitted.

*Enter two other Servingmen,* ABRAHAM *and* BALTHASAR.

SAM. My naked weapon is out; quarrel, I will back thee.

'My naked weapon is out' omitted.

GRE. How? turn thy back and run?

SAM. Fear me not.

GRE. No, marry; I fear thee!

SAM. Let us take the law of our sides; let them begin.

GRE. I will frown as I pass by, and let them take it as they list.

SAM. Nay, as they dare. I will bite my thumb at them, which is disgrace to them if they bear it.

ABR. Do you bite your thumb at us, sir?

SAM. I do bite my thumb, sir.

ABR. Do you bite your thumb at us, sir?

SAM. [*Aside to* GREGORY.] Is the law of our side, if I say ay?

GRE. [*Aside to* SAMPSON.] No.

SAM. No, sir, I do not bite my thumb at you, sir; but I bite my thumb, sir.

GRE. Do you quarrel, sir?

ABR. Quarrel, sir! No, sir.

SAM. But if you do, sir, I am for you. I serve as good a man as you.

ABR. No better?

SAM. Well, sir.

*Enter* BENVOLIO.

GRE. [*Aside to* SAMPSON.] Say 'better'; here comes one of my master's kinsmen.

SAM. Yes, better, sir.

ABR. You lie.

| SAM. Draw, if you be men. Gregory, remember thy swashing blow. [*They fight.* | 'Draw . . . Gregory' omitted.

| BEN. Part, fools! [*Beats down their swords.* | 'Part, fools' omitted.
Put up your swords; you know not what you do.

*Enter* TYBALT.

| TYB. What, art thou drawn among these heartless hinds? | Line 64 omitted.
Turn thee, Benvolio; look upon thy death.

BEN. I do but keep the peace; put up thy sword,
Or manage it to part these men with me.

TYB. What, drawn, and talk of peace! I hate the word,
As I hate hell, all Montagues, and thee.
Have at thee, coward! [*They fight.*

*Enter an* OFFICER, *and three or four* CITIZENS *with clubs or partisans.*

| OFFICER. Clubs, bills, and partisans! Strike; beat them down. | Line 71 is spoken after line 78.

CITIZENS. Down with the Capulets! Down with the Montagues!

*Enter* OLD CAPULET *in his gown, and his* WIFE.

CAP. What noise is this? Give me my long sword, ho!

LADY C. A crutch, a crutch! Why call you for a sword?

CAP. My sword, I say! Old Montague is come,
And flourishes his blade in spite of me.

*Enter* OLD MONTAGUE *and his* WIFE.

MON. Thou villain Capulet!—Hold me not, let me go.

LADY M. Thou shalt not stir one foot to seek a foe.

*Enter* PRINCE ESCALUS, *with his* TRAIN. Line 71 here.

PRIN. Rebellious subjects, enemies to peace,
Profaners of this neighbour-stained steel—
Will they not hear? What, ho! you men, you beasts,
That quench the fire of your pernicious rage
With purple fountains issuing from your veins!
On pain of torture, from those bloody hands
Throw your mistempered weapons to the ground,
And hear the sentence of your moved prince.
Three civil brawls, bred of an airy word,
By thee, old Capulet, and Montague,
Have thrice disturb'd the quiet of our streets
And made Verona's ancient citizens
Cast by their grave beseeming ornaments
To wield old partisans, in hands as old,
Cank'red with peace, to part your cank'red hate.
If ever you disturb our streets again,
Your lives shall pay the forfeit of the peace.
For this time all the rest depart away.
You, Capulet, shall go along with me;
And, Montague, come you this afternoon,
To know our farther pleasure in this case,
| To old Free-town, our common judgment-place. | Line 100 omitted.
Once more, on pain of death, all men depart.
[*Exeunt all but* MONTAGUE, *his* WIFE, *and* BENVOLIO.

| MON. Who set this ancient quarrel new abroach?
Speak, nephew; were you by when it began? | Lines 102–113 omitted.

BEN. Here were the servants of your adversary
And yours, close fighting ere I did approach.
I drew to part them; in the instant came
The fiery Tybalt, with his sword prepar'd;
Which, as he breath'd defiance to my ears,
He swung about his head and cut the winds,
Who, nothing hurt withal, hiss'd him in scorn.
While we were interchanging thrusts and blows,
Came more and more, and fought on part and part,
Till the Prince came, who parted either part.

Lines 102–113 omitted.

LADY M. O, where is Romeo? Saw you him to-day?
Right glad I am he was not at this fray.

BEN. Madam, an hour before the worshipp'd sun
Peer'd forth the golden window of the east,
A troubled mind drew me to walk abroad;
Where, underneath the grove of sycamore
That westward rooteth from this city side,
So early walking did I see your son.
Towards him I made; but he was ware of me
And stole into the covert of the wood.
I, measuring his affections by my own,
Which then most sought where most might not be found,
Being one too many by my weary self,
Pursu'd my humour, not pursuing his,
And gladly shunn'd who gladly fled from me.

SCENE 2
*Interior. Montague's House. Day.*
MONTAGUE, LADY MONTAGUE, BENVOLIO.

Lines 124–128 omitted.

MON. Many a morning hath he there been seen,
With tears augmenting the fresh morning's dew,
Adding to clouds more clouds with his deep sighs;
But all so soon as the all-cheering sun
Should in the farthest east begin to draw
The shady curtains from Aurora's bed,
Away from light steals home my heavy son,
And private in his chamber pens himself,
Shuts up his windows, locks fair daylight out,
And makes himself an artificial night.
Black and portentous must this humour prove,
Unless good counsel may the cause remove.

BEN. My noble uncle, do you know the cause?

MON. I neither know it nor can learn of him.

BEN. Have you importun'd him by any means?

MON. Both by myself and many other friends.
But he, his own affections' counsellor,
Is to himself—I will not say how true;
But to himself so secret and so close,
So far from sounding and discovery,
As is the bud bit with an envious worm,
Ere he can spread his sweet leaves to the air,
Or dedicate his beauty to the sun.
Could we but learn from whence his sorrows grow,
We would as willingly give cure as know.

Lines 145–151 omitted.

*Enter* ROMEO.

BEN. See where he comes. So please you step aside;

ROMEO *does not enter.* For 'See where he comes', read 'Trust me, my lord'.

I'll know his grievance or be much denied.
MON. I would thou wert so happy by thy stay
To hear true shrift. Come, madam, let's away.

Lines 156–157 omitted.

[*Exeunt* MONTAGUE *and his* WIFE.

SCENE 3
*Exterior, Montague's Orchard. Day.*
ROMEO, BENVOLIO

BEN. Good morrow, cousin.
ROM. Is the day so young?
BEN. But new struck nine.
ROM. Ay me! sad hours seem long.
Was that my father that went hence so fast?
BEN. It was. What sadness lengthens Romeo's hours?

Line 160 omitted.
Line 161, 'It was' omitted.

ROM. Not having that which having makes them short.
BEN. In love?
ROM. Out—
BEN. Of love?
ROM. Out of her favour where I am in love.
BEN. Alas that love, so gentle in his view,
Should be so tyrannous and rough in proof!
ROM. Alas that love, whose view is muffled still,
Should without eyes see pathways to his will!
Where shall we dine? O me! What fray was here?
Yet tell me not, for I have heard it all.
Here's much to do with hate, but more with love.
Why then, O brawling love! O loving hate!
O anything, of nothing first create!
O heavy lightness! serious vanity!
Mis-shapen chaos of well-seeming forms!
Feather of lead, bright smoke, cold fire, sick health!
Still-waking sleep, that is not what it is!

Line 179 omitted.

This love feel I, that feel no love in this.
Dost thou not laugh?
BEN. No, coz, I rather weep.
ROM. Good heart, at what?
BEN. At thy good heart's oppression.
ROM. Why, such is love's transgression.
Griefs of mine own lie heavy in my breast,
Which thou wilt propagate, to have it prest
With more of thine. This love that thou hast shown
Doth add more grief to too much of mine own.

Lines 184–187 omitted.

Love is a smoke rais'd with the fume of sighs;
Being purg'd, a fire sparkling in lovers' eyes;
Being vex'd, a sea nourish'd with loving tears.
What is it else? A madness most discreet,
A choking gall, and a preserving sweet.
Farewell, my coz.
BEN. Soft! I will go along;
An if you leave me so, you do me wrong.
ROM. Tut, I have lost myself; I am not here:
This is not Romeo, he's some other where.
BEN. Tell me in sadness who is that you love.
ROM. What, shall I groan and tell thee?
BEN. Groan! Why, no;
But sadly tell me who.
ROM. Bid a sick man in sadness make his will.

Lines 200–201 omitted.

Ah, word ill urg'd to one that is so ill!
In sadness, cousin, I do love a woman.
BEN. I aim'd so near when I suppos'd you lov'd.
ROM. A right good markman! And she's fair I love.
BEN. A right fair mark, fair coz, is soonest hit.
ROM. Well, in that hit you miss: she'll not be hit
With Cupid's arrow. She hath Dian's wit,
And in strong proof of chastity well arm'd,
From Love's weak childish bow she lives unharm'd.
She will not stay the siege of loving terms,
Nor bide th' encounter of assailing eyes,
Nor ope her lap to saint-seducing gold.
O, she is rich in beauty; only poor
That, when she dies, with beauty dies her store.
BEN. Then she hath sworn that she will still live chaste?
ROM. She hath, and in that sparing makes huge waste;
For beauty, starv'd with her severity,
Cuts beauty off from all posterity.
She is too fair, too wise, wisely too fair,
To merit bliss by making me despair.
She hath forsworn to love, and in that vow
Do I live dead that live to tell it now.
BEN. Be rul'd by me: forget to think of her.
ROM. O, teach me how I should forget to think!
BEN. By giving liberty unto thine eyes.
Examine other beauties.
ROM. 'Tis the way
To call hers, exquisite, in question more.
These happy masks that kiss fair ladies' brows,
Being black, puts us in mind they hide the fair.
He that is stricken blind cannot forget
The precious treasure of his eyesight lost.
Show me a mistress that is passing fair,
What doth her beauty serve but as a note
Where I may read who pass'd that passing fair?
Farewell; thou canst not teach me to forget.
BEN. I'll pay that doctrine or else die in debt. [*Exeunt.*

Line 201 omitted.

Line 207 from 'She hath Dian's wit' to line 214 omitted.

Lines 217–220 omitted.

Lines 226–229 omitted.

## SCENE II. *A street.*

*Enter* CAPULET, COUNTY PARIS, *and the* CLOWN, *his servant.*

SCENE 4
*Exterior. Verona. The Square. Day.*

CAP. But Montague is bound as well as I,
In penalty alike; and 'tis not hard, I think,
For men so old as we to keep the peace.
PAR. Of honourable reckoning are you both,
And pity 'tis you liv'd at odds so long.
But now, my lord, what say you to my suit?
CAP. But saying o'er what I have said before:
My child is yet a stranger in the world,
She hath not seen the change of fourteen years;
Let two more summers wither in their pride
Ere we may think her ripe to be a bride.
PAR. Younger than she are happy mothers made.
CAP. And too soon marr'd are those so early made.

Earth hath swallowed all my hopes but she;
She is the hopeful lady of my earth.
But woo her, gentle Paris, get her heart;
My will to her consent is but a part.
And, she agreed, within her scope of choice
Lies my consent and fair according voice.
This night I hold an old accustom'd feast,
Whereto I have invited many a guest,
Such as I love; and you among the store,
One more, most welcome, makes my number more.
At my poor house look to behold this night
Earth-treading stars that make dark heaven light.
Such comfort as do lusty young men feel
When well-apparell'd April on the heel
Of limping winter treads, even such delight
Among fresh female buds shall you this night
Inherit at my house. Hear all, all see,
And like her most whose merit most shall be;
Which on more view of many, mine, being one,
May stand in number, though in reck'ning none.
Come, go with me. [*To* SERVANT, *giving him a paper*.] Go, sirrah, trudge about
Through fair Verona; find those persons out
Whose names are written there, and to them say
My house and welcome on their pleasure stay.
[*Exeunt* CAPULET *and* PARIS.

| Lines 32–33 omitted.

SERV. Find them out whose names are written here! It is written that the shoemaker should meddle with his yard and the tailor with his last, the fisher with his pencil and the painter with his nets; but I am sent to find those persons whose names are here writ, and can never find what names the writing person hath here writ. I must to the learned. In good time! 44

*Enter* BENVOLIO *and* ROMEO.

BEN. Tut, man, one fire burns out another's burning,
One pain is less'ned by another's anguish;
Turn giddy, and be holp by backward turning;
One desperate grief cures with another's languish.
Take thou some new infection to thy eye,
And the rank poison of the old will die.

| For 'holp' read 'helped'.

ROM. Your plantain leaf is excellent for that.
BEN. For what, I pray thee?
ROM. For your broken shin.
BEN. Why, Romeo, art thou mad?
ROM. Not mad, but bound more than a madman is;
Shut up in prison, kept without my food,
Whipt and tormented, and—God-den, good fellow.

| Lines 52–56, 'For what, I pray thee . . . tormented, and', omitted.

SERV. God gi' go'den. I pray, sir, can you read?
ROM. Ay, mine own fortune in my misery.
SERV. Perhaps you have learned it without book. But I pray, can you read anything you see?
ROM. Ay, if I know the letters and the language.
SERV. Ye say honestly; rest you merry!

ROM. Stay, fellow; I can read.
[*He reads the list.*] 'Signior Martino and his wife and daughters; County Anselme and his beauteous sisters; the lady widow of Vitruvio; Signior Placentio and his lovely nieces; Mercutio and his brother Valentine; mine uncle Capulet, his wife, and daughters; my fair niece Rosaline and Livia; Signior Valentio and his cousin Tybalt; Lucio and the lively Helena.'
A fair assembly. [*Gives back the paper.*] Whither should they come?
SERV. Up.
ROM. Whither?
SERV. To supper. To our house.
ROM. Whose house?
SERV. My master's.
ROM. Indeed, I should have ask'd you that before.
SERV. Now I'll tell you without asking: my master is the great rich Capulet; and if you be not of the house of Montagues, I pray come and crush a cup of wine. Rest you merry! [*Exit.*
BEN. At this same ancient feast of Capulet's
Sups the fair Rosaline whom thou so loves,
With all the admired beauties of Verona.
Go thither, and with unattainted eye
Compare her face with some that I shall show,
And I will make thee think thy swan a crow.

*Lines 88–91 omitted.*

ROM. When the devout religion of mine eye
Maintains such falsehood, then turn tears to fires;
And these who, often drown'd, could never die,
Transparent heretics, be burnt for liars!
One fairer than my love! The all-seeing sun
Ne'er saw her match since first the world begun.
BEN. Tut, you saw her fair, none else being by,
Herself pois'd with herself in either eye;
But in that crystal scales let there be weigh'd
Your lady's love against some other maid
That I will show you shining at this feast,
And she shall scant show well that now seems best.
ROM. I'll go along, no such sight to be shown,
But to rejoice in splendour of mine own. [*Exeunt.*

SCENE III. *Capulet's house.*

*Scene 5*
*Interior. Juliet's Chambers. Day.*

*Enter* LADY CAPULET *and* NURSE.

LADY C. Nurse, where's mv daughter? Call her forth to me.
NURSE. Now, by my maidenhead at twelve year old,
I bade her come. What, lamb! what, ladybird!
God forbid! Where's this girl? What, Juliet!

*Enter* JULIET.

JUL. How now, who calls?
NURSE. Your mother.
JUL. Madam, I am here. What is your will?
LADY C. This is the matter. Nurse, give leave awhile,
We must talk in secret. Nurse, come back again;

I have rememb'red me, thou's hear our counsel.
Thou knowest my daughter's of a pretty age.
NURSE. Faith, I can tell her age unto an hour.
LADY C. She's not fourteen.
NURSE. I'll lay fourteen of my teeth—
And yet, to my teen be it spoken, I have but four—
She's not fourteen. How long is it now
To Lammas-tide?
LADY C. A fortnight and odd days.
NURSE. Even or odd, of all days in the year,
Come Lammas Eve at night shall she be fourteen.
Susan and she—God rest all Christian souls!—
Were of an age. Well, Susan is with God;
She was too good for me. But, as I said,
On Lammas Eve at night shall she be fourteen;
That shall she, marry; I remember it well.
'Tis since the earthquake now eleven years;
And she was wean'd—I never shall forget it—
Of all the days of the year, upon that day;
For I had then laid wormwood to my dug,
Sitting in the sun under the dove-house wall;
My lord and you were then at Mantua.
Nay, I do bear a brain. But, as I said,
When it did taste the wormwood on the nipple
Of my dug, and felt it bitter, pretty fool,
To see it tetchy, and fall out with the dug!
Shake, quoth the dove-house. 'Twas no need, I trow,
To bid me trudge.
And since that time it is eleven years;
For then she could stand high-lone; nay, by th' rood,
She could have run and waddled all about;
For even the day before, she broke her brow;
And then my husband—God be with his soul!
'A was a merry man—took up the child.
'Yea,' quoth he 'dost thou fall upon thy face?
Thou wilt fall backward when thou hast more wit,
Wilt thou not, Jule?' And, by my holidam,
The pretty wretch left crying, and said 'Ay'.
To see, now, how a jest shall come about!
I warrant, an I should live a thousand years,
I never should forget it: 'Wilt thou not, Jule?' quoth he;
And, pretty fool, it stinted, and said 'Ay'.
LADY C. Enough of this; I pray thee hold thy peace.
| NURSE. Yes, madam. Yet I cannot choose but laugh
To think it should leave crying and say 'Ay'.
And yet, I warrant, it had upon it brow
A bump as big as a young cock'rel's stone—
A perilous knock; and it cried bitterly.
'Yea,' quoth my husband 'fall'st upon thy face?
Thou wilt fall backward when thou comest to age;
Wilt thou not, Jule?' It stinted, and said 'Ay'.
JUL. And stint thou too, I pray thee, nurse, say I.
NURSE. Peace, I have done. God mark thee to his grace!
Thou wast the prettiest babe that e'er I nurs'd;

| Add after 'Yes, madam':
LADY C. Juliet!

An I might live to see thee married once,
I have my wish.

LADY C. Marry, that 'marry' is the very theme
I came to talk of. Tell me, daughter Juliet,
How stands your dispositions to be married?

JUL. It is an honour that I dream not of.

NURSE. An honour! Were not I thine only nurse,
I would say thou hadst suck'd wisdom from thy teat.

LADY C. Well, think of marriage now. Younger than you,
Here in Verona, ladies of esteem,
Are made already mothers. By my count,
I was your mother much upon these years
That you are now a maid. Thus, then, in brief:
The valiant Paris seeks you for his love.

NURSE. A man, young lady! lady, such a man
As all the world—why, he's a man of wax.

LADY C. Verona's summer hath not such a flower.

NURSE. Nay, he's a flower; in faith, a very flower.

LADY C. What say you? Can you love the gentleman?
This night you shall behold him at our feast;
Read o'er the volume of young Paris' face,
And find delight writ there with beauty's pen;
Examine every married lineament,
And see how one another lends content;
And what obscur'd in this fair volume lies
Find written in the margent of his eyes.
This precious book of love, this unbound lover,
To beautify him, only lacks a cover.
The fish lives in the sea, and 'tis much pride
For fair without the fair within to hide.
That book in many's eyes doth share the glory
That in gold clasps locks in the golden story;
So shall you share all that he doth possess,
By having him making yourself no less.

NURSE. No less! Nay, bigger; women grow by men.

LADY C. Speak briefly, can you like of Paris' love?

JUL. I'll look to like, if looking liking move;
But no more deep will I endart mine eye
Than your consent gives strength to make it fly.

*Enter a* SERVANT.

SERV. Madam, the guests are come, supper serv'd up, you call'd, my young lady asked for, the nurse curs'd in the pantry, and everything in extremity. I must hence to wait; I beseech you, follow straight.

LADY C. We follow thee. [*Exit* SERVANT.] Juliet, the County stays.

NURSE. Go, girl, seek happy nights to happy days. [*Exeunt.*

## SCENE IV. *A street.*

SCENE 6
*Exterior. Verona. A Street. Night.*

*Enter* ROMEO, MERCUTIO, BENVOLIO, *with five or six other* MASKERS; TORCH-BEARERS.

| ROM. What, shall this speech be spoke for our excuse?
Or shall we on without apology?

| Line 1 omitted.
For 'Or' read 'But'.

BEN. The date is out of such prolixity.
We'll have no Cupid hoodwink'd with a scarf,
Bearing a Tartar's painted bow of lath,
Scaring the ladies like a crow-keeper;
Nor no without-book prologue, faintly spoke
After the prompter, for our entrance;
But, let them measure us by what they will,
We'll measure them a measure, and be gone.

Lines 4–8 omitted.

ROM. Give me a torch; I am not for this ambling;
Being but heavy, I will bear the light.
MER. Nay, gentle Romeo, we must have you dance
ROM. Not I, believe me. You have dancing shoes
With nimble soles: I have a soul of lead
So stakes me to the ground I cannot move.
MER. You are a lover; borrow Cupid's wings
And soar with them above a common bound.
ROM. I am too sore enpierced with his shaft
To soar with his light feathers; and so bound
I cannot bound a pitch above dull woe.
Under love's heavy burden do I sink.
MER. And to sink in it should you burden love;
Too great oppression for a tender thing.
ROM. Is love a tender thing? It is too rough,
Too rude, too boist'rous, and it pricks like thorn.
MER. If love be rough with you, be rough with love;
Prick love for pricking, and you beat love down.
Give me a case to put my visage in. [*Putting on a mask.*
A visor for a visor! What care I
What curious eye doth quote deformities?
Here are the beetle brows shall blush for me.
BEN. Come, knock and enter; and no sooner in
But every man betake him to his legs.
ROM. A torch for me. Let wantons, light of heart,
Tickle the senseless rushes with their heels;
For I am proverb'd with a grandsire phrase;
I'll be a candle-holder and look on;
The game was ne'er so fair, and I am done.
MER. Tut, dun's the mouse, the constable's own word;
If thou art Dun, we'll draw thee from the mire
Of this sir-reverence love, wherein thou stickest
Up to the ears. Come, we burn daylight, ho!
ROM. Nay, that's not so.
MER. I mean, sir, in delay
We waste our lights in vain—like lights by day.
Take our good meaning, for our judgment sits
Five times in that ere once in our five wits.

Lines 35–47 omitted.

ROM. And we mean well in going to this mask;
But 'tis no wit to go.
MER. Why, may one ask?
ROM. I dreamt a dream to-night.
MER. And so did I.
ROM. Well, what was yours?
MER. That dreamers often lie.
ROM. In bed asleep, while they do dream things true.

MER. O, then I see Queen Mab hath been with you.
She is the fairies' midwife, and she comes
In shape no bigger than an agate stone
On the fore-finger of an alderman,
Drawn with a team of little atomies
Athwart men's noses as they lie asleep ;
Her waggon-spokes made of long spinners' legs ;
The cover, of the wings of grasshoppers ;
Her traces, of the smallest spider's web ;
Her collars, of the moonshine's wat'ry beams ;
Her whip, of cricket's bone ; the lash, of film ;
Her waggoner, a small grey-coated gnat,
Not half so big as a round little worm
Prick'd from the lazy finger of a maid.
Her chariot is an empty hazel-nut,
Made by the joiner squirrel or old grub,
Time out o' mind the fairies' coachmakers.
And in this state she gallops night by night
Through lovers' brains, and then they dream of love ;
O'er courtiers' knees, that dream on curtsies straight ;
O'er lawyers' fingers, who straight dream on fees ;
O'er ladies' lips, who straight on kisses dream,
Which oft the angry Mab with blisters plagues,
Because their breaths with sweetmeats tainted are.
Sometimes she gallops o'er a courtier's nose,
And then dreams he of smelling out a suit ;
And sometime comes she with a tithe-pig's tail,
Tickling a parson's nose as 'a lies asleep,
Then dreams he of another benefice.
Sometime she driveth o'er a soldier's neck,
And then dreams he of cutting foreign throats,
Of breaches, ambuscadoes, Spanish blades,
Of healths five fathoms deep ; and then anon
Drums in his ear, at which he starts and wakes,
And, being thus frighted, swears a prayer or two,
And sleeps again. This is that very Mab
That plats the manes of horses in the night ;
And bakes the elf-locks in foul sluttish hairs,
Which once untangled much misfortune bodes.
This is the hag, when maids lie on their backs,
That presses them and learns them first to bear,
Making them women of good carriage.
This is she—

ROM. Peace, peace, Mercutio, peace !
Thou talk'st of nothing.

MER. True, I talk of dreams,
Which are the children of an idle brain,
Begot of nothing but vain fantasy ;
Which is as thin of substance as the air,
And more inconstant than the wind, who woos
Even now the frozen bosom of the north,
And, being anger'd, puffs away from thence,
Turning his side to the dew-dropping south.

BEN. This wind you talk of blows us from ourselves :

Supper is done, and we shall come too late.
ROM. I fear, too early; for my mind misgives
Some consequence, yet hanging in the stars,
Shall bitterly begin his fearful date
With this night's revels and expire the term
Of a despised life clos'd in my breast,
By some vile forfeit of untimely death.
But He that hath the steerage of my course
Direct my sail! On, lusty gentlemen.
BEN. Strike, drum. [*They march about the stage. Exeunt.*

SCENE V. *Capulet's house.*

*Enter the* MASKERS. SERVINGMEN *come forth with napkins.*

1 SERV. Where's Potpan, that he helps not to take away? He shift a trencher! He scrape a trencher!
2 SERV. When good manners shall lie all in one or two men's hands, and they unwash'd too, 'tis a foul thing.
1 SERV. Away with the join-stools, remove the court-cubbert, look to the plate. Good thou, save me a piece of marchpane; and as thou loves me let the porter let in Susan Grindstone and Nell. Antony, and Potpan!
2 SERV. Ay, boy, ready. 9
1 SERV. You are look'd for and call'd for, ask'd for and sought for, in the great chamber.
3 SERV. We cannot be here and there too. Cheerly, boys! Be brisk a while, and the longer liver take all! [SERVANTS *retire.*

*Enter* CAPULET, *with all the* GUESTS *and* GENTLEWOMEN *to the* MASKERS.

CAP. Welcome, gentlemen! Ladies that have their toes
Unplagu'd with corns will have a bout with you.
Ah ha, my mistresses! which of you all
Will now deny to dance? She that makes dainty,
She I'll swear hath corns; am I come near ye now?
Welcome, gentlemen! I have seen the day
That I have worn a visor and could tell
A whispering tale in a fair lady's ear,
Such as would please. 'Tis gone, 'tis gone, 'tis gone!
You are welcome, gentlemen. Come, musicians, play.
A hall, a hall! give room; and foot it, girls.
[*Music plays, and they dance.*
More light, you knaves; and turn the tables up,
And quench the fire, the room is grown too hot.
Ah, sirrah, this unlook'd for sport comes well.
Nay, sit, nay, sit, good cousin Capulet,
For you and I are past our dancing days.
How long is't now since last yourself and I
Were in a mask?
2 CAP. By'r Lady, thirty years.
CAP. What, man? 'tis not so much, 'tis not so much.
'Tis since the nuptial of Lucentio,
Come Pentecost as quickly as it will,
Some five and twenty years; and then we mask'd.
2 CAP. 'Tis more, 'tis more: his son is elder, sir;
His son is thirty.

SCENE 7
*Interior. Capulet's house. Main Hall entrance and Scullery. Night.*
Line 1 from 'He shift' to line 7 '. . . and Nell' omitted.

2 SERVANT for 3 SERVANT. After line 13 2 SERV. continues: 'Look to the plate. Look to the plate. Good thou, save me a piece of marchpane.'

CAP. Will you tell me that?
His son was but a ward two years ago.
ROM. [*To a* SERVANT.] What lady's that which doth enrich the hand
Of yonder knight?
SERV. I know not, sir.
ROM. O, she doth teach the torches to burn bright!
It seems she hangs upon the cheek of night
As a rich jewel in an Ethiop's ear—
Beauty too rich for use, for earth too dear!
So shows a snowy dove trooping with crows
As yonder lady o'er her fellows shows.
The measure done, I'll watch her place of stand,
And, touching hers, make blessed my rude hand.
Did my heart love till now? Forswear it, sight;
For I ne'er saw true beauty till this night.
TYB. This, by his voice, should be a Montague.
Fetch me my rapier, boy. What, dares the slave
Come hither, cover'd with an antic face,
To fleer and scorn at our solemnity?
Now, by the stock and honour of my kin,
To strike him dead I hold it not a sin.
CAP. Why, how now, kinsman! Wherefore storm you so?
TYB. Uncle, this is a Montague, our foe;
A villain, that is hither come in spite
To scorn at our solemnity this night.
CAP. Young Romeo, is it?
TYB. 'Tis he, that villain Romeo.
CAP. Content thee, gentle coz, let him alone.
'A bears him like a portly gentleman;
And, to say truth, Verona brags of him
To be a virtuous and well-govern'd youth.
I would not for the wealth of all this town
Here in my house do him disparagement.
Therefore be patient, take no note of him;
It is my will; the which if thou respect,
Show a fair presence and put off these frowns,
An ill-beseeming semblance for a feast.
TYB. It fits, when such a villain is a guest.
I'll not endure him.
CAP. He shall be endur'd.
What, goodman boy! I say he shall. Go to;
Am I the master here or you? Go to.
You'll not endure him! God shall mend my soul!
You'll make a mutiny among my guests!
You will set cock-a-hoop! You'll be the man!
TYB. Why, uncle, 'tis a shame.
CAP. Go to, go to;
You are a saucy boy. Is't so, indeed?
This trick may chance to scathe you. I know what:
You must contrary me. Marry, 'tis time.—
Well said, my hearts!—You are a princox; go.
Be quiet, or—More light, more light!—For shame!
I'll make you quiet. What!—Cheerly, my hearts!

Lines 48–49 omitted.

Line 52 omitted.

TYB. Patience perforce with wilful choler meeting
Makes my flesh tremble in their different greeting.
I will withdraw; but this intrusion shall,
Now seeming sweet, convert to bitt'rest gall. [*Exit.*
ROM. [*To* JULIET.] If I profane with my unworthiest hand
This holy shrine, the gentle fine is this:
My lips, two blushing pilgrims, ready stand
To smooth that rough touch with a tender kiss.
JUL. Good pilgrim, you do wrong your hand too much,
Which mannerly devotion shows in this;
For saints have hands that pilgrims' hands do touch,
And palm to palm is holy palmers' kiss.
ROM. Have not saints lips, and holy palmers too?
JUL. Ay, pilgrim, lips that they must use in pray'r.
ROM. O, then, dear saint, let lips do what hands do!
They pray; grant thou, lest faith turn to despair.
JUL. Saints do not move, though grant for prayers' sake.
ROM. Then move not while my prayer's effect I take.
Thus from my lips by thine my sin is purg'd. [*Kissing her.*
JUL. Then have my lips the sin that they have took.
ROM. Sin from my lips? O trespass sweetly urg'd!
Give me my sin again. [*Kissing her.*
JUL. You kiss by th' book.
NURSE. Madam, your mother craves a word with you.
ROM. What is her mother?
NURSE. Marry, bachelor,
Her mother is the lady of the house,
And a good lady, and a wise and virtuous.
I nurs'd her daughter that you talk'd withal.
I tell you, he that can lay hold of her
Shall have the chinks.
ROM. Is she a Capulet?
O dear account! my life is my foe's debt.
BEN. Away, be gone; the sport is at the best.
ROM. Ay, so I fear; the more is my unrest.
CAP. Nay, gentlemen, prepare not to be gone;
We have a trifling foolish banquet towards.
Is it e'en so? Why, then I thank you all;
I thank you, honest gentlemen; good night.
More torches here! [*Exeunt* MASKERS.] Come on then, let's to bed.
Ah, sirrah, by my fay, it waxes late;
I'll to my rest. [*Exeunt all but* JULIET *and* NURSE.

Lines 123–125 omitted from '[*Exeunt* MASKERS]'. *All remain on stage.*

JUL. Come hither, nurse. What is yond gentleman?
NURSE. The son and heir of old Tiberio.
JUL. What's he that now is going out of door?
NURSE. Marry, that I think be young Petruchio.
JUL. What's he that follows there, that would not dance?
NURSE. I know not.
JUL. Go ask his name.—If he be married,
My grave is like to be my wedding bed.
NURSE. His name is Romeo, and a Montague;
The only son of your great enemy.
JUL. My only love sprung from my only hate!
Too early seen unknown, and known too late!

Prodigious birth of love it is to me,
That I must love a loathed enemy.
NURSE. What's this? What's this?
JUL. A rhyme I learnt even now
Of one I danc'd withal. [*One calls within* 'Juliet'.
NURSE. Anon, anon!
Come, let's away; the strangers all are gone. [*Exeunt.*

Stage direction omitted.
'Anon, anon' omitted.
'The strangers all are gone' omitted.

## ACT TWO

## PROLOGUE

*Enter* CHORUS.

Now old desire doth in his death-bed lie,
And young affection gapes to be his heir;
That fair for which love groan'd for and would die,
With tender Juliet match'd, is now not fair.
Now Romeo is belov'd, and loves again,
Alike bewitched by the charm of looks;
But to his foe suppos'd he must complain,
And she steal love's sweet bait from fearful hooks.
Being held a foe, he may not have access
To breathe such vows as lovers use to swear;
And she as much in love, her means much less
To meet her new beloved any where.
But passion lends them power, time means, to meet,
Temp'ring extremities with extreme sweet. [*Exit.*

### SCENE I. *A lane by the wall of Capulet's orchard.*

SCENE 8
*Exterior. A Lane by the Wall of Capulet's Orchard. Night.*

*Enter* ROMEO.

ROM. Can I go forward when my heart is here?
Turn back, dull earth, and find thy centre out.
[*He climbs the wall and leaps down within it.*

*Enter* BENVOLIO *with* MERCUTIO.

BEN. Romeo! my cousin, Romeo! Romeo!
MER. He is wise,
And, on my life, hath stol'n him home to bed.
BEN. He ran this way, and leapt this orchard wall.
Call, good Mercutio.
MER. Nay, I'll conjure too.
Romeo! humours! madman! passion! lover!
Appear thou in the likeness of a sigh;
Speak but one rhyme and I am satisfied;
Cry but 'Ay me!' pronounce but 'love' and 'dove';
Speak to my gossip Venus one fair word,
One nickname for her purblind son and heir,
Young Adam Cupid, he that shot so trim
When King Cophetua lov'd the beggar-maid!
He heareth not, he stirreth not, he moveth not;

Lines 13–14 omitted.

The ape is dead, and I must conjure him.
I conjure thee by Rosaline's bright eyes,
By her high forehead and her scarlet lip,
By her fine foot, straight leg, and quivering thigh,
And the demesnes that there adjacent lie,
That in thy likeness thou appear to us.

BEN. An if he hear thee, thou wilt anger him.

MER. This cannot anger him : 'twould anger him
To raise a spirit in his mistress' circle
Of some strange nature, letting it there stand
Till she had laid it and conjur'd it down ;
That were some spite. My invocation
Is fair and honest : in his mistress' name,
I conjure only but to raise up him.

BEN. Come, he hath hid himself among these trees
To be consorted with the humorous night :
Blind is his love, and best befits the dark.

MER. If love be blind, love cannot hit the mark.
Now will he sit under a medlar tree,
And wish his mistress were that kind of fruit
As maids call medlars when they laugh alone.
O Romeo, that she were, O that she were
An open et cetera, thou a pop'rin pear !
Romeo, good night. I'll to my truckle bed ;
This field-bed is too cold for me to sleep.
Come, shall we go ?

BEN. Go, then ; for 'tis in vain
To seek him here that means not to be found. [*Exeunt.*

SCENE II. *Capulet's orchard.*

*Enter* ROMEO.

SCENE 9
*Exterior. Capulet's Orchard. Night.*
Line 1 is spoken at the end of the previous scene.

ROM. He jests at scars that never felt a wound.

*Enter* JULIET *above at a window.*

But, soft ! What light through yonder window breaks ?
It is the east, and Juliet is the sun.
Arise, fair sun, and kill the envious moon,
Who is already sick and pale with grief
That thou her maid art far more fair than she.
Be not her maid, since she is envious ;
Her vestal livery is but sick and green,
And none but fools do wear it ; cast it off.
It is my lady ; O, it is my love !
O that she knew she were !
She speaks, yet she says nothing. What of that ?
Her eye discourses ; I will answer it.
I am too bold, 'tis not to me she speaks ;
Two of the fairest stars in all the heaven,
Having some business, do entreat her eyes
To twinkle in their spheres till they return.
What if her eyes were there, they in her head ?
The brightness of her cheek would shame those stars,
As daylight doth a lamp ; her eyes in heaven

Would through the airy region stream so bright
That birds would sing, and think it were not night.
See how she leans her cheek upon her hand!
O that I were a glove upon that hand,
That I might touch that cheek!

JUL. Ay me!

ROM. She speaks.
O, speak again, bright angel, for thou art
As glorious to this night, being o'er my head,
As is a winged messenger of heaven
Unto the white-upturned wond'ring eyes
Of mortals that fall back to gaze on him,
When he bestrides the lazy-pacing clouds
And sails upon the bosom of the air.

JUL. O Romeo, Romeo! wherefore art thou Romeo?
Deny thy father and refuse thy name;
Or, if thou wilt not, be but sworn my love,
And I'll no longer be a Capulet.

ROM. [*Aside.*] Shall I hear more, or shall I speak at this?

JUL. 'Tis but thy name that is my enemy;
Thou art thyself, though not a Montague.
What's Montague? It is nor hand, nor foot,
Nor arm, nor face, nor any other part
Belonging to a man. O, be some other name!
What's in a name? That which we call a rose
By any other name would smell as sweet;
So Romeo would, were he not Romeo call'd,
Retain that dear perfection which he owes
Without that title. Romeo, doff thy name;
And for thy name, which is no part of thee,
Take all myself.

ROM. I take thee at thy word:
Call me but love, and I'll be new baptiz'd;
Henceforth I never will be Romeo.

JUL. What man art thou, that, thus bescreen'd in night,
So stumblest on my counsel?

ROM. By a name
I know not how to tell thee who I am:
My name, dear saint, is hateful to myself,
Because it is an enemy to thee;
Had I it written, I would tear the word.

JUL. My ears have yet not drunk a hundred words
Of thy tongue's uttering, yet I know the sound
Art thou not Romeo, and a Montague?

ROM. Neither, fair maid, if either thee dislike.

JUL. How cam'st thou hither, tell me, and wherefore?
The orchard walls are high and hard to climb;
And the place death, considering who thou art,
If any of my kinsmen find thee here.

ROM. With love's light wings did I o'erperch these walls,
For stony limits cannot hold love out;
And what love can do, that dares love attempt.
Therefore thy kinsmen are no stop to me.

JUL. If they do see thee, they will murder thee.

ROM. Alack, there lies more peril in thine eye
Than twenty of their swords; look thou but sweet,
And I am proof against their enmity.
JUL. I would not for the world they saw thee here.
ROM. I have night's cloak to hide me from their eyes;
And but thou love me, let them find me here.
My life were better ended by their hate
Than death prorogued wanting of thy love.
JUL. By whose direction found'st thou out this place?
ROM. By love, that first did prompt me to enquire;
He lent me counsel, and I lent him eyes.
I am no pilot; yet, wert thou as far
As that vast shore wash'd with the farthest sea,
I should adventure for such merchandise.
JUL. Thou knowest the mask of night is on my face,
Else would a maiden blush bepaint my cheek
For that which thou hast heard me speak to-night.
Fain would I dwell on form, fain, fain deny
What I have spoke; but farewell compliment!
Dost thou love me? I know thou wilt say ay,
And I will take thy word; yet, if thou swear'st,
Thou mayst prove false; at lovers' perjuries
They say Jove laughs. O gentle Romeo,
If thou dost love, pronounce it faithfully.
Or, if thou think'st I am too quickly won,
I'll frown, and be perverse, and say thee nay,
So thou wilt woo; but else, not for the world.
In truth, fair Montague, I am too fond;
And therefore thou mayst think my haviour light;
But trust me, gentleman, I'll prove more true
Than those that have more cunning to be strange.
I should have been more strange, I must confess,
But that thou overheard'st, ere I was ware,
My true love's passion. Therefore pardon me,
And not impute this yielding to light love,
Which the dark night hath so discovered.
ROM. Lady, by yonder blessed moon I vow,
That tips with silver all these fruit-tree tops—
JUL. O, swear not by the moon, th' inconstant moon,
That monthly changes in her circled orb,
Lest that thy love prove likewise variable.
ROM. What shall I swear by?
JUL. Do not swear at all;
Or, if thou wilt, swear by thy gracious self,
Which is the god of my idolatry,
| And I'll believe thee.
ROM. If my heart's dear love—
JUL. Well, do not swear. Although I joy in thee,
I have no joy of this contract to-night:
It is too rash, too unadvis'd, too sudden;
Too like the lightning, which doth cease to be
Ere one can say 'It lightens'. Sweet, good night!
This bud of love, by summer's ripening breath,
May prove a beauteous flow'r when next we meet.

| 'And I'll believe thee' omitted.

Good night, good night! As sweet repose and rest
Come to thy heart as that within my breast!
ROM. O, wilt thou leave me so unsatisfied?
JUL. What satisfaction canst thou have to-night?
ROM. Th' exchange of thy love's faithful vow for mine.
JUL. I gave thee mine before thou didst request it;
And yet I would it were to give again.
ROM. Wouldst thou withdraw it? For what purpose, love?
JUL. But to be frank, and give it thee again.
And yet I wish but for the thing I have.
My bounty is as boundless as the sea,
My love as deep: the more I give to thee,
The more I have, for both are infinite. [NURSE *calls within.*
I hear some noise within. Dear love, adieu!—
Anon, good nurse!—Sweet Montague, be true.
Stay but a little, I will come again. [*Exit.*
ROM. O blessed, blessed night! I am afeard,
Being in night, all this is but a dream,
Too flattering-sweet to be substantial.

*Re-enter* JULIET *above.*

JUL. Three words, dear Romeo, and good night indeed.
If that thy bent of love be honourable,
Thy purpose marriage, send me word to-morrow,
By one that I'll procure to come to thee,
Where and what time thou wilt perform the rite;
And all my fortunes at thy foot I'll lay,
And follow thee, my lord, throughout the world.
NURSE. [*Within.*] Madam!
JUL. I come anon.—But if thou meanest not well,
I do beseech thee—
NURSE. [*Within.*] Madam!
JUL. By and by, I come—
To cease thy suit, and leave me to my grief.
To-morrow will I send.
ROM. So thrive my soul—
JUL. A thousand times good night! [*Exit.*
ROM. A thousand times the worse, to want thy light.
Love goes toward love as school-boys from their books;
But love from love, toward school with heavy looks.

*Re-enter* JULIET *above.*

JUL. Hist! Romeo, hist!—O for a falc'ner's voice,
To lure this tassel-gentle back again!
Bondage is hoarse, and may not speak aloud;
Else would I tear the cave where Echo lies,
And make her airy tongue more hoarse than mine
With repetition of my Romeo's name.
Romeo!
ROM. It is my soul that calls upon my name.
How silver-sweet sound lovers' tongues by night,
Like softest music to attending ears!
JUL. Romeo!
ROM. My dear?

*Rebecca Saire as Juliet*

*Joseph O'Conor as Friar Lawrence with Romeo (Patrick Ryecart)*

*John Gielgud as Chorus*

*Patrick Ryecart as Romeo*

*Alan Rickman as Tybalt (left) and Anthony Andrews as Mercutio (right)*

*From left to right: Mercutio (on the ground), Romeo, Benvolio (Christopher Strauli) and an attendant*

*Celia Johnson as the Nurse*

*Michael Hordern as Capulet and Jacqueline Hill as Lady Capulet with Juliet*

JUL. At what o'clock to-morrow
Shall I send to thee?
ROM. By the hour of nine.
JUL. I will not fail. 'Tis twenty years till then.
I have forgot why I did call thee back.
ROM. Let me stand here till thou remember it.
JUL. I shall forget, to have thee still stand there,
Rememb'ring how I love thy company.
ROM. And I'll still stay, to have thee still forget,
Forgetting any other home but this.
JUL. 'Tis almost morning. I would have thee gone;
And yet no farther than a wanton's bird,
That lets it hop a little from her hand,
Like a poor prisoner in his twisted gyves,
And with a silk thread plucks it back again,
So loving-jealous of his liberty.
ROM. I would I were thy bird.
JUL. Sweet, so would I.
Yet I should kill thee with much cherishing.
Good night, good night! Parting is such sweet sorrow
That I shall say good night till it be morrow. [*Exit.*
ROM. Sleep dwell upon thine eyes, peace in thy breast!
Would I were sleep and peace, so sweet to rest!
Hence will I to my ghostly father's cell,
His help to crave and my dear hap to tell. [*Exit.*

Lines 189–190 omitted.

## SCENE III. *Friar Lawrence's cell.*

*Enter* FRIAR LAWRENCE *with a basket.*

SCENE 10
*Exterior. Outside Friar Lawrence's Cell.*

FRI. L. The gray-ey'd morn smiles on the frowning night,
Check'ring the eastern clouds with streaks of light;
And fleckel'd darkness like a drunkard reels
From forth day's path and Titan's fiery wheels.
Now, ere the sun advance his burning eye
The day to cheer and night's dank dew to dry,
I must up-fill this osier cage of ours
With baleful weeds and precious-juiced flowers.
The earth that's nature's mother is her tomb;
What is her burying grave, that is her womb.
And from her womb children of divers kind
We sucking on her natural bosom find;
Many for many virtues excellent,
None but for some, and yet all different.
O, mickle is the powerful grace that lies
In plants, herbs, stones, and their true qualities;
For nought so vile that on the earth doth live
But to the earth some special good doth give;
Nor aught so good but, strain'd from that fair use
Revolts from true birth, stumbling on abuse:
Virtue itself turns vice, being misapplied,
And vice sometime's by action dignified.
Within the infant rind of this weak flower
Poison hath residence, and medicine power;
For this, being smelt, with that part cheers each part;

Lines 13–14 omitted.

Lines 21–22 omitted.

Being tasted, slays all senses with the heart.
Two such opposed kings encamp them still
In man as well as herbs—grace and rude will;
And where the worser is predominant,
Full soon the canker death eats up that plant.

*Enter* ROMEO.

ROM. Good morrow, father!
FRI. L. Benedicite!
What early tongue so sweet saluteth me?
Young son, it argues a distempered head
So soon to bid good morrow to thy bed.
Care keeps his watch in every old man's eye,
And where care lodges sleep will never lie;
But where unbruised youth with unstuff'd brain
Doth couch his limbs, there golden sleep doth reign.
Therefore thy earliness doth me assure
Thou art uprous'd with some distemp'rature;
Or if not so, then here I hit it right—
Our Romeo hath not been in bed to-night.

Lines 35–40 omitted.

ROM. That last is true; the sweeter rest was mine.
FRI. L. God pardon sin! Wast thou with Rosaline?
ROM. With Rosaline, my ghostly father? No;
I have forgot that name, and that name's woe.
FRI. L. That's my good son; but where hast thou been then?
ROM. I'll tell thee ere thou ask it me again.
I have been feasting with mine enemy;
Where, on a sudden, one hath wounded me
That's by me wounded; both our remedies
Within thy help and holy physic lies.
I bear no hatred, blessed man, for, lo,
My intercession likewise steads my foe.
FRI. L. Be plain, good son, and homely in thy drift;
Riddling confession finds but riddling shrift.
ROM. Then plainly know my heart's dear love is set
On the fair daughter of rich Capulet.
As mine on hers, so hers is set on mine;
And all combin'd, save what thou must combine
By holy marriage. When, and where, and how,
We met, we woo'd, and made exchange of vow,
I'll tell thee as we pass; but this I pray,
That thou consent to marry us to-day.
FRI. L. Holy Saint Francis! What a change is here
Is Rosaline, that thou didst love so dear,
So soon forsaken? Young men's love, then, lies
Not truly in their hearts, but in their eyes.
Jesu Maria, what a deal of brine
Hath wash'd thy sallow cheeks for Rosaline!
How much salt water thrown away in waste,
To season love, that of it doth not taste!
The sun not yet thy sighs from heaven clears,
Thy old groans yet ring in mine ancient ears;
Lo, here upon thy cheek the stain doth sit
Of an old tear that is not wash'd off yet.

Lines 73–74 omitted.

If e'er thou wast thyself, and these woes thine,
Thou and these woes were all for Rosaline.
And art thou chang'd? Pronounce this sentence, then:
Women may fall, when there's no strength in men.
ROM. Thou chid'st me oft for loving Rosaline.
FRI. L. For doting, not for loving, pupil mine.
ROM. And bad'st me bury love.
FRI. L. Not in a grave
To lay one in, another out to have.
ROM. I pray thee chide me not; her I love now
Doth grace for grace and love for love allow;
The other did not so.
FRI. L. O, she knew well
Thy love did read by rote that could not spell.
But come, young waverer, come, go with me,
In one respect I'll thy assistant be;
For this alliance may so happy prove
To turn your household's rancour to pure love.
ROM. O, let us hence; I stand on sudden haste.
FRI. L. Wisely and slow; they stumble that run fast. [*Exeunt.*

SCENE IV. *A street.*

SCENE II
*Exterior. Verona. The Square. Day.*

*Enter* BENVOLIO *and* MERCUTIO.

MER. Where the devil should this Romeo be?
Came he not home to-night?
BEN. Not to his father's; I spoke with his man.
MER. Why, that same pale hard-hearted wench, that Rosaline,
Torments him so that he will sure run mad.
BEN. Tybalt, the kinsman to old Capulet,
Hath sent a letter to his father's house.
MER. A challenge, on my life.
BEN. Romeo will answer it.
MER. Any man that can write may answer a letter.
BEN. Nay, he will answer the letter's master, how he dares, being dared.

MER. Alas, poor Romeo, he is already dead: stabb'd with a white wench's black eye; run through the ear with a love-song; the very pin of his heart cleft with the blind bow-boy's butt-shaft. And is he a man to encounter Tybalt?

BEN. Why, what is Tybalt?

MER. More than Prince of Cats. O, he's the courageous captain of compliments. He fights as you sing prick-song: keeps time, distance, and proportion; he rests his minim rests, one, two, and the third in your bosom; the very butcher of a silk button, a duellist, a duellist; a gentleman of the very first house, of the first and second cause. Ah, the immortal passado! the punto reverso! the hay!—

BEN. The what?

MER. The pox of such antic, lisping, affecting fantasticoes; these new tuners of accent!—'By Jesu, a very good blade! a very tall man! a very good whore!' Why, is not this a lamentable thing, grandsire, that we should be thus afflicted with these strange flies, these fashion-mongers, these pardon me's, who stand so much on the new form that they cannot sit at ease on the old bench? O, their bones, their bones!

*Enter* ROMEO.

BEN. Here comes Romeo, here comes Romeo.

MER. Without his roe, like a dried herring. O flesh, flesh, how art thou fishified! Now is he for the numbers that Petrarch flow'd in; Laura, to his lady, was a kitchen-wench—marry, she had a better love to berhyme her; Dido, a dowdy; Cleopatra, a gipsy; Helen and Hero, hildings and harlots; Thisbe, a gray eye or so, but not to the purpose—Signior Romeo, bon jour! There's a French salutation to your French slop. You gave us the counterfeit fairly last night.

Lines 38–42, 'Now is he . . . to the purpose', omitted.

ROM. Good morrow to you both. What counterfeit did I give you?

'Good morrow to you both' is spoken 2 lines earlier after 'French slop'.

MER. The slip, sir, the slip; can you not conceive?

ROM. Pardon, good Mercutio; my business was great, and in such a case as mine a man may strain courtesy.

MER. That's as much as to say, such a case as yours constrains a man to bow in the hams.

ROM. Meaning, to curtsy.

MER. Thou hast most kindly hit it.

ROM. A most courteous exposition.

MER. Nay, I am the very pink of courtesy.

ROM. Pink for flower.

MER. Right.

ROM. Why, then is my pump well flower'd.

MER. Sure wit! Follow me this jest now till thou hast worn out thy pump, that, when the single sole of it is worn, the jest may remain, after the wearing, solely singular.

ROM. O single-sol'd jest, solely singular for the singleness!

Lines 60–63, 'Sure wit . . . singleness', omitted.

MER. Come between us, good Benvolio; my wits faints.

ROM. Swits and spurs, swits and spurs; or I'll cry a match.

MER. Nay, if our wits run the wild-goose chase, I am done; for thou hast more of the wild goose in one of thy wits than, I am sure, I have in my whole five. Was I with you there for the goose?

Lines 69–83, 'Swits and spurs . . . broad goose', omitted.

ROM. Thou wast never with me for anything when thou wast not there for the goose.

MER. I will bite thee by the ear for that jest.

ROM. Nay, good goose, bite not.

MER. Thy wit is a very bitter sweeting; it is a most sharp sauce.

ROM. And is it not then well serv'd in to a sweet goose?

MER. O, here's a wit of cheveril, that stretches from an inch narrow to an ell broad!

ROM. I stretch it out for that word 'broad', which, added to the goose, proves thee far and wide a broad goose.

MER. Why, is not this better now than groaning for love? Now art thou sociable, now art thou Romeo; now art thou what thou art by art as well as by nature; for this drivelling love is like a great natural that runs lolling up and down to hide his bauble in a hole.

BEN. Stop there, stop there.

MER. Thou desirest me to stop in my tale against the hair.

BEN. Thou wouldst else have made thy tale large.

Lines 91–95 omitted.

MER. O, thou art deceiv'd: I would have made it short; for I was come to the whole depth of my tale, and meant, indeed, to occupy the argument no longer.

Lines 91–95 omitted.

ROM. Here's goodly gear!

*Enter* NURSE *and her man,* PETER.

MER. A sail, a sail!

BEN. Two, two; a shirt and a smock.

NURSE. Peter!

PETER. Anon.

NURSE. My fan, Peter.

MER. Good Peter, to hide her face; for her fan's the fairer face.

NURSE. God ye good morrow, gentlemen.

MER. God ye good den, fair gentlewoman.

NURSE. Is it good den?

MER. 'Tis no less, I tell ye; for the bawdy hand of the dial is now upon the prick of noon.

NURSE. Out upon you! What a man are you?

ROM. One, gentlewoman, that God hath made himself to mar.

NURSE. By my troth, it is well said. 'For himself to mar' quoth 'a! Gentlemen, can any of you tell me where I may find the young Romeo?

ROM. I can tell you; but young Romeo will be older when you have found him than he was when you sought him. I am the youngest of that name, for fault of a worse.

NURSE. You say well.

MER. Yea, is the worst well? Very well took, i' faith; wisely, wisely.

NURSE. If you be he, sir, I desire some confidence with you.

BEN. She will indite him to some supper.

MER. A bawd, a bawd, a bawd! So ho!

ROM. What hast thou found?

MER. No hare, sir; unless a hare, sir, in a lenten pie, that is something stale and hoar ere it be spent. [*He walks by them and sings.*

An old hare hoar,
And an old hare hoar,
Is very good meat in Lent;
But a hare that is hoar
Is too much for a score,
When it hoars ere it be spent.

Romeo, will you come to your father's? We'll to dinner thither.

ROM. I will follow you.

MER. Farewell, ancient lady; farewell, [*sings.*] lady, lady, lady.

[*Exeunt* MERCUTIO *and* BENVOLIO.

NURSE. I pray you, sir, what saucy merchant was this that was so full of his ropery?

ROM. A gentleman, nurse, that loves to hear himself talk, and will speak more in a minute than he will stand to in a month.

NURSE. An 'a speak anything against me, I'll take him down, an 'a were lustier than he is, and twenty such Jacks; and if I cannot, I'll find those that shall. Scurvy knave! I am none of his flirt-gills; I am none of his skains-mates. And thou must stand by too, and suffer every knave to use me at his pleasure?

PET. I saw no man use you at his pleasure; if I had, my weapon should quickly have been out, I warrant you. I dare draw as soon as another man, if I see occasion in a good quarrel, and the law on my side.

NURSE. Now, afore God, I am so vex'd that every part about me quivers. Scurvy knave!—Pray you, sir, a word; and as I told you, my young lady bid me enquire you out; what she bid me say I will keep to myself. But first let me tell ye, if ye should lead her in a fool's paradise, as they say, it were a very gross kind of behaviour, as they say; for the gentlewoman is young; and, therefore, if you should deal double with her, truly it were an ill thing to be off'red to any gentlewoman, and very weak dealing.

Lines 162–172, 'for the gentlewoman . . . gentleman-like offer', omitted.

ROM. Nurse, commend me to thy lady and mistress. I protest unto thee—

NURSE. Good heart, and, i' faith, I will tell her as much. Lord, Lord! she will be a joyful woman.

ROM. What wilt thou tell her, nurse? Thou dost not mark me.

NURSE. I will tell her, sir, that you do protest; which, as I take it, is a gentleman-like offer.

ROM. Bid her devise
Some means to come to shrift this afternoon;
And there she shall at Friar Lawrence' cell
Be shriv'd and married. Here is for thy pains.

Lines 177–187, 'Here is for thy pains . . . Farewell', omitted.

NURSE. No, truly, sir; not a penny.

ROM. Go to; I say you shall.

NURSE. This afternoon, sir? Well, she shall be there.

ROM. And stay, good nurse—behind the abbey wall
Within this hour my man shall be with thee,
And bring thee cords made like a tackled stair;
Which to the high top-gallant of my joy
Must be my convoy in the secret night.
Farewell; be trusty, and I'll quit thy pains.
Farewell; commend me to thy mistress.

NURSE. Now God in heaven bless thee!—
Hark you, sir.

ROM. What say'st thou, my dear nurse?

Lines 189–192 omitted.

NURSE. Is your man secret? Did you ne'er hear say
Two may keep counsel, putting one away?

ROM. I warrant thee my man's as true as steel.

NURSE. Well, sir. My mistress is the sweetest lady—Lord, Lord! when 'twas a little prating thing! O, there is a nobleman in town, one Paris, that would fain lay knife aboard; but she, good soul, had as lief see a toad, a very toad, as see him. I anger her sometimes, and tell her that Paris is the properer man; but, I'll warrant you, when I say so she looks as pale as any clout in the versal world. Doth not rosemary and Romeo begin both with a letter?

'Well, sir' omitted.

Lines 200–206, from 'Doth not rosemary', omitted.

ROM. Ay, nurse; what of that? Both with an R.

NURSE. Ah, mocker! that's the dog's name. R is for the—no, I know it begins with some other letter. And she hath the prettiest sententious of it, of you and rosemary, that it would do you good to hear it.

ROM. Commend me to thy lady.

NURSE. Ay, a thousand times.—Peter!
PET. Anon.
NURSE. [*Handing him her fan.*] Before and apace. [*Exeunt.*

SCENE V. *Capulet's orchard.*

*Enter* JULIET.

SCENE 12
*Exterior, Capulet's Orchard. Day.*

JUL. The clock struck nine when I did send the nurse;
In half an hour she promis'd to return.
Perchance she cannot meet him—that's not so.
O, she is lame! Love's heralds should be thoughts,
Which ten times faster glide than the sun's beams
Driving back shadows over louring hills;
Therefore do nimble-pinion'd doves draw Love,
And therefore hath the wind-swift Cupid wings.
Now is the sun upon the highmost hill
Of this day's journey; and from nine till twelve
Is three long hours, yet she is not come.
Had she affections and warm youthful blood,
She would be as swift in motion as a ball;
My words would bandy her to my sweet love,
And his to me.
But old folks—many feign as they were dead;
Unwieldy, slow, heavy, and pale as lead.

Lines 7–8 omitted.

*Enter* NURSE *and* PETER.

O God, she comes! O honey nurse, what news?
Hast thou met with him? Send thy man away.
NURSE. Peter, stay at the gate. [*Exit* PETER.
JUL. Now, good sweet nurse—O Lord, why look'st thou sad?
Though news be sad, yet tell them merrily;
If good, thou shamest the music of sweet news
By playing it to me with so sour a face.
NURSE. I am aweary, give me leave a while;
Fie, how my bones ache! What a jaunce have I had!
JUL. I would thou hadst my bones and I thy news.
Nay, come, I pray thee speak; good, good nurse, speak.
NURSE. Jesu, what haste? Can you not stay a while?
Do you not see that I am out of breath?
JUL. How art thou out of breath, when thou hast breath
To say to me that thou art out of breath?
The excuse that thou dost make in this delay
Is longer than the tale thou dost excuse.
Is thy news good or bad? Answer to that;
Say either, and I'll stay the circumstance.
Let me be satisfied, is't good or bad?
NURSE. Well, you have made a simple choice; you know not how to choose a man. Romeo! no, not he; though his face be better than any man's, yet his leg excels all men's; and for a hand, and a foot, and a body, though they be not to be talk'd on, yet they are past compare. He is not the flower of courtesy, but I'll warrant him as gentle as a lamb. Go thy ways, wench; serve God. What, have you din'd at home?
JUL. No, no. But all this did I know before.
What says he of our marriage? What of that?
NURSE. Lord, how my head aches! What a head have I!

It beats as it would fall in twenty pieces.
My back a t' other side—ah, my back, my back!
Beshrew your heart for sending me about
To catch my death with jauncing up and down!

JUL. I' faith, I am sorry that thou art not well.
Sweet, sweet, sweet nurse, tell me, what says my love?

NURSE. Your love says like an honest gentleman, and a courteous, and a kind, and a handsome, and, I warrant, a virtuous—Where is your mother?

JUL. Where is my mother! Why, she is within;
Where should she be? How oddly thou repliest!
'Your love says like an honest gentleman,
Where is your mother?'

NURSE. O God's lady dear!
Are you so hot? Marry, come up, I trow;
Is this the poultice for my aching bones?
Henceforward, do your messages yourself.

JUL. Here's such a coil! Come, what says Romeo?

NURSE. Have you got leave to go to shrift to-day?

JUL. I have.

NURSE. Then hie you hence to Friar Lawrence' cell;
There stays a husband to make you a wife.
Now comes the wanton blood up in your cheeks;
They'll be in scarlet straight at any news.
Hie you to church; I must another way,
To fetch a ladder, by the which your love
Must climb a bird's nest soon when it is dark.
I am the drudge, and toil in your delight;
But you shall bear the burden soon at night.
Go; I'll to dinner; hie you to the cell.

JUL. Hie to high fortune! Honest nurse, farewell. [*Exeunt.*

## SCENE VI. *Friar Lawrence's cell.*

SCENE 13
*Interior. Friar Lawrence's Cell. Day.*

*Enter* FRIAR LAWRENCE *and* ROMEO.

FRI. L. So smile the heavens upon this holy act
That after-hours with sorrow chide us not!

ROM. Amen, amen! But come what sorrow can,
It cannot countervail the exchange of joy
That one short minute gives me in her sight.
Do thou but close our hands with holy words,
Then love-devouring death do what he dare;
It is enough I may but call her mine.

FRI. L. These violent delights have violent ends,
And in their triumph die; like fire and powder,
Which, as thy kiss, consume. The sweetest honey
Is loathsome in his own deliciousness,
And in the taste confounds the appetite.
Therefore love moderately: long love doth so;
Too swift arrives as tardy as too slow.

Lines 10–15 omitted.

*Enter* JULIET.

Here comes the lady. O, so light a foot

Will ne'er wear out the everlasting flint.
A lover may bestride the gossamer
That idles in the wanton summer air
And yet not fall, so light is vanity.

JUL. Good even to my ghostly confessor.

FRI. L. Romeo shall thank thee, daughter, for us both.

JUL. As much to him, else is his thanks too much.

Lines 23–34 omitted.

ROM. Ah, Juliet, if the measure of thy joy
Be heap'd like mine, and that thy skill be more
To blazon it, then sweeten with thy breath
This neighbour air, and let rich music's tongue
Unfold the imagin'd happiness that both
Receive in either by this dear encounter.

JUL. Conceit, more rich in matter than in words,
Brags of his substance, not of ornament.
They are but beggars that can count their worth;
But my true love is grown to such excess
I cannot sum up sum of half my wealth.

FRI. L. Come, come with me, and we will make short work;
For, by your leaves, you shall not stay alone
Till holy church incorporate two in one. [*Exeunt.*

For 'Come, come with me', read 'Come, come here to me'. FRIAR LAWRENCE continues: 'Deus Israel conjungat vos: et ipse sit vobiscum, qui misertus est duobus unicis: et nunc, Domine . . .'

## ACT THREE

### SCENE I. *A public place.*

*Enter* MERCUTIO, BENVOLIO, PAGE, *and* SERVANTS.

SCENE 14
*Exterior. Verona. The Square. Day.*

BEN. I pray thee, good Mercutio, let's retire.
The day is hot, the Capulets abroad,
And if we meet we shall not scape a brawl;
For now, these hot days, is the mad blood stirring.

MER. Thou art like one of these fellows that, when he enters the confines of a tavern, claps me his sword upon the table, and says 'God send me no need of thee!' and by the operation of the second cup draws him on the drawer, when, indeed, there is no need.

BEN. Am I like such a fellow?

MER. Come, come, thou art as hot a Jack in thy mood as any in Italy; and as soon moved to be moody, and as soon moody to be moved.

BEN. And what to?

MER. Nay, an there were two such, we should have none shortly, for one would kill the other. Thou! why, thou wilt quarrel with a man that hath a hair more or a hair less in his beard than thou hast. Thou wilt quarrel with a man for cracking nuts, having no other reason but because thou hast hazel eyes. What eye but such an eye would spy out such a quarrel? Thy head is as full of quarrels as an egg is full of meat; and yet thy head hath been beaten as addle as an egg for quarrelling. Thou has quarrell'd with a man for coughing in the street, because he hath wakened thy dog that hath lain asleep in the sun. Didst thou not fall out with a tailor for wearing his new doublet before Easter?

With another for tying his new shoes with old riband? And yet thou wilt tutor me from quarrelling!

BEN. An I were so apt to quarrel as thou art, any man should buy the fee simple of my life for an hour and a quarter.

MER. The fee simple! O simple!

Lines 30–32 omitted.

*Enter* TYBALT *and* OTHERS.

BEN. By my head, here comes the Capulets.

MER. By my heel, I care not.

TYB. Follow me close, for I will speak to them.
Gentlemen, good den; a word with one of you.

MER. And but one word with one of us? Couple it with something; make it a word and a blow.

TYB. You shall find me apt enough to that, sir, an you will give me occasion.

MER. Could you not take some occasion without giving?

TYB. Mercutio, thou consortest with Romeo.

MER. Consort! What, dost thou make us minstrels? An thou make minstrels of us, look to hear nothing but discords. Here's my fiddlestick; here's that shall make you dance. Zounds, consort!

BEN. We talk here in the public haunt of men;
Either withdraw unto some private place,
Or reason coldly of your grievances,
Or else depart; here all eyes gaze on us.

MER. Men's eyes were made to look, and let them gaze;
I will not budge for no man's pleasure, I.

*Enter* ROMEO.

TYB. Well, peace be with you, sir. Here comes my man.

MER. But I'll be hang'd, sir, if he wear your livery.
Marry, go before to field, he'll be your follower;
Your worship in that sense may call him man.

TYB. Romeo, the love I bear thee can afford
No better term than this: thou art a villain.

ROM. Tybalt, the reason that I have to love thee
Doth much excuse the appertaining rage
To such a greeting. Villain am I none;
Therefore, farewell; I see thou knowest me not.

TYB. Boy, this shall not excuse the injuries
That thou hast done me; therefore turn and draw.

ROM. I do protest I never injur'd thee,
But love thee better than thou canst devise
Till thou shalt know the reason of my love;
And so, good Capulet—which name I tender
As dearly as mine own—be satisfied.

MER. O calm, dishonourable, vile submission!
Alla stoccata carries it away. [*Draws.*
Tybalt, you rat-catcher, will you walk?

TYB. What wouldst thou have with me?

MER. Good King of Cats, nothing but one of your nine lives; that I mean to make bold withal, and, as you shall use me hereafter, dry-beat the rest of the eight. Will you pluck your sword out

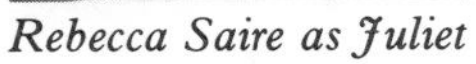

*Rebecca Saire as Juliet*

*Michael Hordern as Capulet*

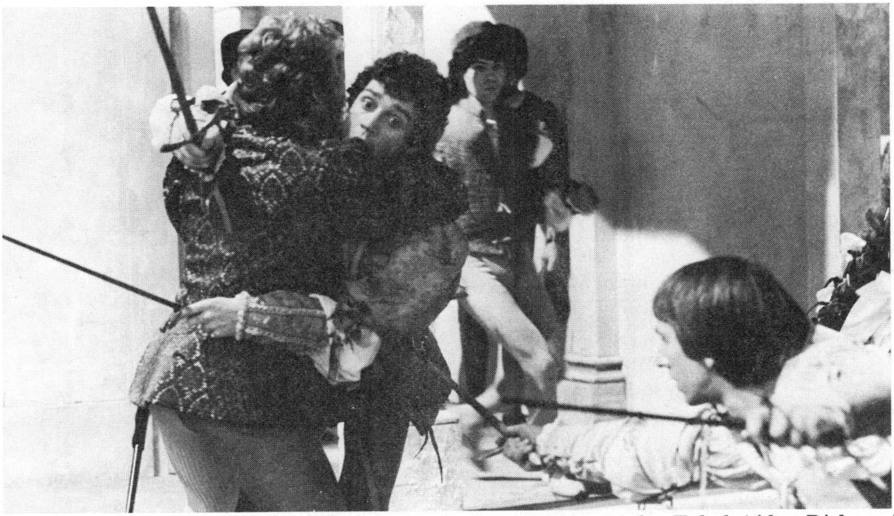

*Romeo (Patrick Ryecart) supports Mercutio (Anthony Andrews) after Tybalt (Alan Rickman) has thrust him through*

of his pilcher by the ears? Make haste, lest mine be about your ears ere it be out.

TYB. I am for you. [*Draws.*

'I am for you' omitted.

ROM. Gentle Mercutio, put thy rapier up.
MER. Come, sir, your passado. [*They fight.*
ROM. Draw, Benvolio; beat down their weapons.
Gentlemen, for shame, forbear this outrage!
Tybalt! Mercutio! the Prince expressly hath
Forbid this bandying in Verona streets.
Hold, Tybalt! Good Mercutio!

[TYBALT *under* ROMEO'S *arm thrusts* MERCUTIO *in, and flies with his friends.*

MER. I am hurt.
A plague a both your houses! I am sped.
Is he gone and hath nothing?
BEN. What, art thou hurt?
MER. Ay, ay, a scratch, a scratch; marry, 'tis enough.
Where is my page? Go, villain, fetch a surgeon. [*Exit* PAGE.
ROM. Courage, man; the hurt cannot be much.

MER. No, 'tis not so deep as a well, nor so wide as a church door, but 'tis enough, 'twill serve. Ask for me to-morrow, and you shall find me a grave man. I am peppered, I warrant, for this world. A plague a both your houses! Zounds, a dog, a rat, a mouse, a cat, to scratch a man to death! A braggart, a rogue, a villain, that fights by the book of arithmetic! Why the devil came you between us? I was hurt under your arm.

ROM. I thought all for the best.
MER. Help me into some house, Benvolio, or I shall faint.
A plague a both your houses!
They have made worms' meat of me.
I have it, and soundly too—Your houses!

[*Exeunt* MERCUTIO *and* BENVOLIO.

ROM. This gentleman, the Prince's near ally,
My very friend, hath got this mortal hurt
In my behalf; my reputation stain'd
With Tybalt's slander—Tybalt, that an hour
Hath been my cousin. O sweet Juliet,
Thy beauty hath made me effeminate,
And in my temper soft'ned valour's steel!

Lines 106–110, 'This gentleman . . . my cousin', omitted.

*Re-enter* BENVOLIO.

BEN. O Romeo, Romeo, brave Mercutio is dead!
That gallant spirit hath aspir'd the clouds,
Which too untimely here did scorn the earth.
ROM. This day's black fate on moe days doth depend;
This but begins the woe others must end.

*Re-enter* TYBALT.

BEN. Here comes the furious Tybalt back again.
ROM. Alive in triumph and Mercutio slain!
Away to heaven respective lenity,
And fire-ey'd fury be my conduct now!
Now, Tybalt, take the 'villain' back again
That late thou gav'st me; for Mercutio's soul

*Romeo chases Tybalt through the streets.*
SCENE 15
*Exterior. Verona. The The Streets. Day.*
TYBALT, ROMEO.

Is but a little way above our heads,
Staying for thine to keep him company.
Either thou or I, or both, must go with him.

TYB. Thou, wretched boy, that didst consort him here,
Shalt with him hence.

ROM. This shall determine that.

*[They fight ;* TYBALT *falls.*

BEN. Romeo, away, be gone.
The citizens are up, and Tybalt slain.
Stand not amaz'd. The Prince will doom thee death
If thou art taken. Hence, be gone, away!

ROM. O, I am fortune's fool!

BEN. Why dost thou stay? *[Exit* ROMEO.

*Enter* CITIZENS.

1 CIT. Which way ran he that kill'd Mercutio?
Tybalt, that murderer, which way ran he?

BEN. There lies that Tybalt.

1 CIT. Up, sir, go with me;
I charge thee in the Prince's name, obey.

Lines 134–135 and 136–137 1 CIT.'s lines spoken by WATCHMAN.

*Enter* PRINCE, *attended ;* MONTAGUE, CAPULET, *their* WIVES, *and* ALL.

SCENE 16
*Interior. Prince's Throne Room. Day.*

PRIN. Where are the vile beginners of this fray?

BEN. O noble Prince, I can discover all
The unlucky manage of this fatal brawl:
There lies the man, slain by young Romeo,
That slew thy kinsman, brave Mercutio.

LADY C. Tybalt, my cousin! O my brother's child!
O Prince! O husband! O, the blood is spill'd
Of my dear kinsman! Prince, as thou art true,
For blood of ours shed blood of Montague.
O cousin, cousin!

'O my brother's child! O Prince! O husband!' omitted.

'O cousin, cousin' omitted.

PRIN. Benvolio, who began this bloody fray?

BEN. Tybalt, here slain, whom Romeo's hand did slay;
Romeo that spoke him fair, bid him bethink
How nice the quarrel was, and urg'd withal
Your high displeasure. All this, uttered
With gentle breath, calm look, knees humbly bow'd,
Could not take truce with the unruly spleen
Of Tybalt, deaf to peace, but that he tilts
With piercing steel at bold Mercutio's breast;
Who, all as hot, turns deadly point to point,
And, with a martial scorn, with one hand beats
Cold death aside, and with the other sends
It back to Tybalt, whose dexterity
Retorts it. Romeo he cries aloud
'Hold, friends! friends, part!' and, swifter than his tongue,
His agile arm beats down their fatal points,
And 'twixt them rushes; underneath whose arm
An envious thrust from Tybalt hit the life
Of stout Mercutio; and then Tybalt fled;
But by and by comes back to Romeo,
Who had but newly entertain'd revenge,
And to't they go like lightning; for ere I
Could draw to part them was stout Tybalt slain;

For 'here slain' read 'now slain'.

Lines 150–172 omitted.

And as he fell did Romeo turn and fly.
This is the truth, or let Benvolio die.

Lines 150–172 omitted.

LADY C. He is a kinsman to the Montague,
Affection makes him false, he speaks not true;
Some twenty of them fought in this black strife,
And all those twenty could but kill one life.
I beg for justice, which thou, Prince, must give:
Romeo slew Tybalt, Romeo must not live.

PRIN. Romeo slew him; he slew Mercutio.
Who now the price of his dear blood doth owe?

MON. Not Romeo, Prince; he was Mercutio's friend;
His fault concludes but what the law should end,
The life of Tybalt.

PRIN. And for that offence,
Immediately we do exile him hence.
I have an interest in your hate's proceeding,
My blood for your rude brawls doth lie a-bleeding;
But I'll amerce you with so strong a fine
That you shall all repent the loss of mine.
I will be deaf to pleading and excuses,
Nor tears nor prayers shall purchase out abuses;
Therefore use none. Let Romeo hence in haste,
Else when he is found that hour is his last.
Bear hence this body, and attend our will:
Mercy but murders, pardoning those that kill. [*Exeunt.*

'Bear hence this body, and' omitted.

## SCENE II. *Capulet's orchard.*

*Enter* JULIET.

SCENE 17
*Exterior. Capulet's Orchard. Night.*
JULIET

JUL. Gallop apace, you fiery-footed steeds
Towards Phœbus' lodging; such a waggoner
As Phaethon would whip you to the west,
And bring in cloudy night immediately.
Spread thy close curtain, love-performing night,
That runaways' eyes may wink, and Romeo
Leap to these arms, untalk'd of and unseen.
Lovers can see to do their amorous rites
By their own beauties; or if love be blind,
It best agrees with night. Come, civil night,
Thou sober-suited matron, all in black,
And learn me how to lose a winning match,
Play'd for a pair of stainless maidenhoods;
Hood my unmann'd blood, bating in my cheeks,
With thy black mantle, till strange love, grown bold,
Think true love acted simple modesty.
Come, night; come, Romeo; come, thou day in night;
For thou wilt lie upon the wings of night
Whiter than new snow on a raven's back.
Come, gentle night, come, loving black-brow'd night,
Give me my Romeo; and, when he shall die,
Take him and cut him out in little stars,
And he will make the face of heaven so fine
That all the world will be in love with night,
And pay no worship to the garish sun.

O, I have bought the mansion of a love,
But not possess'd it ; and though I am sold,
Not yet enjoy'd. So tedious is this day
As is the night before some festival
To an impatient child that hath new robes,
And may not wear them. O, here comes my nurse,

'O, here comes my nurse' omitted.

*Enter* NURSE *with cords.*

And she brings news ; and every tongue that speaks
But Romeo's name speaks heavenly eloquence.
Now, nurse, what news ? What hast thou there ? The cords
That Romeo bid thee fetch ?

Lines 32–33 omitted.

NURSE. Ay, ay, the cords. [*Throws them down.*
JUL. Ay, me ! what news ? Why dost thou wring thy hands ?
NURSE. Ah, well-a-day ! he's dead, he's dead, he's dead.
We are undone, lady, we are undone.
Alack the day ! he's gone, he's kill'd, he's dead.

Line 37 omitted.

JUL. Can heaven be so envious ?
NURSE. Romeo can,
Though heaven cannot. O Romeo, Romeo !
Who ever would have thought it ? Romeo !
JUL. What devil art thou that dost torment me thus ?
This torture should be roar'd in dismal hell.
Hath Romeo slain himself ? Say thou but ' I '
And that bare vowel I shall poison more
Than the death-darting eye of cockatrice.
I am not I if there be such an ' I ' ;
Or those eyes shut that makes thee answer ' I '.
If he be slain, say ' I ' ; or if not, ' No ' ;
Brief sounds determine of my weal or woe.

Lines 48–49 omitted.

NURSE. I saw the wound, I saw it with mine eyes—
God save the mark !—here on his manly breast.
A piteous corse, a bloody piteous corse ;
Pale, pale as ashes, all bedaub'd in blood,
All in gore-blood. I swounded at the sight.
JUL. O, break, my heart ! poor bankrupt, break at once !
To prison, eyes ; ne'er look on liberty.
Vile earth, to earth resign ; end motion here ;
And thou and Romeo press one heavy bier !
NURSE. O Tybalt, Tybalt, the best friend I had !
O courteous Tybalt ! honest gentleman !
That ever I should live to see thee dead !
JUL. What storm is this that blows so contrary ?
Is Romeo slaught'red, and is Tybalt dead ?
My dearest cousin and my dearer lord ?
Then, dreadful trumpet, sound the general doom ;
For who is living if those two are gone ?
NURSE. Tybalt is gone, and Romeo banished ;
Romeo that kill'd him, he is banished.
JUL. O God ! Did Romeo's hand shed Tybalt's blood ?
NURSE. It did, it did ; alas the day, it did !
JUL. O serpent heart, hid with a flow'ring face !
Did ever dragon keep so fair a cave ?
Beautiful tyrant ! fiend angelical !

Dove-feather'd raven! wolfish-ravening lamb!
Despised substance of divinest show!
Just opposite to what thou justly seem'st,
A damned saint, an honourable villain!
O nature, what hadst thou to do in hell,
When thou didst bower the spirit of a fiend
In mortal paradise of such sweet flesh?
Was ever book containing such vile matter
So fairly bound? O, that deceit should dwell
In such a gorgeous palace!

NURSE. There's no trust,
No faith, no honesty in men; all perjur'd,
All forsworn, all naught, all dissemblers.
Ah, where's my man? Give me some aqua vitæ.
These griefs, these woes, these sorrows, make me old.
Shame come to Romeo!

JUL. Blister'd be thy tongue
For such a wish! He was not born to shame:
Upon his brow shame is asham'd to sit;
For 'tis a throne where honour may be crown'd
Sole monarch of the universal earth.
O, what a beast was I to chide at him!

NURSE. Will you speak well of him that kill'd your cousin?

JUL. Shall I speak ill of him that is my husband?
Ah, poor my lord, what tongue shall smooth thy name,
When I, thy three-hours wife, have mangled it?
But wherefore, villain, didst thou kill my cousin?
That villain cousin would have kill'd my husband.
Back, foolish tears, back to your native spring;
Your tributary drops belong to woe,
Which you, mistaking, offer up to joy.
My husband lives that Tybalt would have slain,
And Tybalt's dead that would have slain my husband.
All this is comfort; wherefore weep I then?
Some word there was, worser than Tybalt's death,
That murd'red me; I would forget it fain,
But, O, it presses to my memory
Like damned guilty deeds to sinners' minds:
'Tybalt is dead, and Romeo banished'.
That 'banished', that one word 'banished',
Hath slain ten thousand Tybalts. Tybalt's death
Was woe enough, if it had ended there;
Or if sour woe delights in fellowship
And needly will be rank'd with other griefs,
Why followed not, when she said 'Tybalt's dead',
Thy father or thy mother, nay, or both,
Which modern lamentation might have mov'd?
But, with a rear-ward following Tybalt's death,
'Romeo is banished'—to speak that word
Is father, mother, Tybalt, Romeo, Juliet,
All slain, all dead. 'Romeo is banished'—
There is no end, no limit, measure, bound,
In that word's death; no words can that woe sound.
Where is my father and my mother, nurse?

Lines 116–117 omitted.

Lines 120–121 omitted.

NURSE. Weeping and wailing over Tybalt's corse.
Will you go to them? I will bring you thither.
JUL. Wash they his wounds with tears! Mine shall be spent,
When theirs are dry, for Romeo's banishment.
Take up those cords. Poor ropes, you are beguil'd,
Both you and I, for Romeo is exil'd;
He made you for a highway to my bed,
But I, a maid, die maiden-widowed.
Come, cords; come, nurse; I'll to my wedding-bed;
And death, not Romeo, take my maidenhead!
NURSE. Hie to your chamber; I'll find Romeo
To comfort you. I wot well where he is.
Hark ye, your Romeo will be here at night.
I'll to him; he is hid at Lawrence' cell.
JUL. O, find him! give this ring to my true knight,
And bid him come to take his last farewell. [*Exeunt.*

Lines 138–143 omitted.

SCENE III. *Friar Lawrence's cell.*

SCENE 18
*Interior. Friar Lawrence's Cell. Night.*

*Enter* FRIAR LAWRENCE.

FRI. L. Romeo, come forth; come forth, thou fearful man;
Affliction is enamour'd of thy parts,
And thou art wedded to calamity.

*Enter* ROMEO.

ROM. Father, what news? What is the Prince's doom?
What sorrow craves acquaintance at my hand
That I yet know not?
FRI. L. Too familiar
Is my dear son with such sour company;
I bring thee tidings of the Prince's doom.
ROM. What less than doomsday is the Prince's doom?
FRI. L. A gentler judgment vanish'd from his lips—
Not body's death, but body's banishment.
ROM. Ha, banishment! Be merciful, say 'death';
For exile hath more terror in his look,
Much more than death. Do not say 'banishment'.

Lines 13–14 omitted.

FRI. L. Here from Verona art thou banished.
Be patient, for the world is broad and wide.
ROM. There is no world without Verona walls,
But purgatory, torture, hell itself.
Hence banished is banish'd from the world,
And world's exile is death. Then 'banished'
Is death mis-term'd; calling death 'banished',
Thou cut'st my head off with a golden axe,
And smilest upon the stroke that murders me.
FRI. L. O deadly sin! O rude unthankfulness!
Thy fault our law calls death; but the kind Prince,
Taking thy part, hath rush'd aside the law,
And turn'd that black word death to banishment.
This is dear mercy, and thou seest it not.
ROM. 'Tis torture, and not mercy; heaven is here
Where Juliet lives, and every cat, and dog,
And little mouse, every unworthy thing,

Live here in heaven and may look on her;
But Romeo may not. More validity,
More honourable state, more courtship lives
In carrion flies than Romeo. They may seize
On the white wonder of dear Juliet's hand,
And steal immortal blessing from her lips;
| Who, even in pure and vestal modesty,
| Still blush, as thinking their own kisses sin;
But Romeo may not—he is banished.
This may flies do, when I from this must fly;
They are free men, but I am banished.
And sayest thou yet that exile is not death?
Hadst thou no poison mix'd, no sharp-ground knife,
No sudden mean of death, though ne'er so mean,
But 'banished' to kill me—'banished'?
O friar, the damned use that word in hell;
Howling attends it; how hast thou the heart,
Being a divine, a ghostly confessor,
A sin-absolver, and my friend profess'd,
To mangle me with that word 'banished'?

| Lines 38–39 omitted.

FRI. L. Thou fond mad man, hear me a little speak.
ROM. O, thou wilt speak again of banishment.
FRI. L. I'll give thee armour to keep off that word;
Adversity's sweet milk, philosophy,
To comfort thee, though thou art banished.
ROM. Yet 'banished'? Hang up philosophy;
Unless philosophy can make a Juliet,
Displant a town, reverse a prince's doom,
It helps not, it prevails not. Talk no more.
FRI. L. O, then I see that madmen have no ears.
ROM. How should they, when that wise men have no eyes?
FRI. L. Let me dispute with thee of thy estate.
ROM. Thou canst not speak of that thou dost not feel.
Wert thou as young as I, Juliet thy love,
An hour but married, Tybalt murdered,
Doting like me, and like me banished,
Then mightst thou speak, then mightst thou tear thy hair,
And fall upon the ground, as I do now,
Taking the measure of an unmade grave. [*Knocking within.*
| FRI. L. Arise; one knocks. Good Romeo, hide thyself.
ROM. Not I; unless the breath of heart-sick groans,
Mist-like, enfold me from the search of eyes. [*Knocking.*
| FRI. L. Hark how they knock! Who's there? Romeo, arise;
Thou wilt be taken.—Stay awhile.—Stand up; [*Knocking.*
Run to my study.—By and by.—God's will,
What simpleness is this!—I come, I come. [*Knocking.*
Who knocks so hard? Whence come you? What's your will?

| 'Arise, one knocks' omitted.

| 'Who's there?' omitted.

NURSE. [*Within.*] Let me come in and you shall know my errand;
I come from Lady Juliet.
FRI. L. Welcome, then.

*Enter* NURSE.

NURSE. O holy friar, O, tell me, holy friar,
Where's my lady's lord, where's Romeo?

FRI. L. There on the ground, with his own tears made drunk.
NURSE. O, he is even in my mistress' case,
Just in her case!
FRI. L. O woeful sympathy | 'sympathy' omitted.
Piteous predicament!
NURSE. Even so lies she,
Blubb'ring and weeping, weeping and blubb'ring.
Stand up, stand up; stand, an you be a man;
For Juliet's sake, for her sake, rise and stand;
Why should you fall into so deep an O?
ROM. Nurse!
NURSE. Ah, sir! ah, sir! Well, death's the end of all.
ROM. Spakest thou of Juliet? How is it with her?
Doth not she think me an old murderer,
Now I have stain'd the childhood of our joy
With blood remov'd but little from her own?
Where is she? and how doth she? and what says
My conceal'd lady to our cancell'd love?
NURSE. O, she says nothing, sir, but weeps and weeps;
And now falls on her bed, and then starts up,
And Tybalt calls; and then on Romeo cries,
And then down falls again.
ROM. As if that name,
Shot from the deadly level of a gun, | Line 103 omitted.
Did murder her; as that name's cursed hand
Murder'd her kinsman. O, tell me, friar, tell me,
In what vile part of this anatomy
Doth my name lodge? Tell me that I may sack
The hateful mansion. [*Drawing his sword.*
FRI. L. Hold thy desperate hand.
Art thou a man? Thy form cries out thou art:
Thy tears are womanish; thy wild acts denote
The unreasonable fury of a beast.
Unseemly woman in a seeming man! | Lines 112–113 omitted.
And ill-beseeming beast in seeming both!
Thou hast amaz'd me. By my holy order,
I thought thy disposition better temper'd.
Hast thou slain Tybalt? Wilt thou slay thyself?
And slay thy lady that in thy life lives,
By doing damned hate upon thyself?
Why railest thou on thy birth, the heaven, and earth | Lines 119–134 omitted.
Since birth, and heaven, and earth, all three do meet
In thee at once; which thou at once wouldst lose.
Fie, fie! thou shamest thy shape, thy love, thy wit
Which, like a usurer, abound'st in all,
And usest none in that true use indeed
Which should bedeck thy shape, thy love, thy wit.
Thy noble shape is but a form of wax,
Digressing from the valour of a man;
Thy dear love sworn but hollow perjury,
Killing that love which thou hast vow'd to cherish;
Thy wit, that ornament to shape and love,
Misshapen in the conduct of them both,
Like powder in a skilless soldier's flask,

Is set afire by thine own ignorance,
And thou dismemb'red with thine own defence.
What, rouse thee, man! Thy Juliet is alive,
For whose dear sake thou wast but lately dead;
There art thou happy. Tybalt would kill thee,
But thou slewest Tybalt; there art thou happy too.
The law, that threat'ned death, becomes thy friend,
And turns it to exile; there art thou happy.
A pack of blessings lights upon thy back;
Happiness courts thee in her best array;
But, like a misbehav'd and sullen wench,
Thou pout'st upon thy fortune and thy love.
Take heed, take heed, for such die miserable.
Go, get thee to thy love, as was decreed,
Ascend her chamber, hence and comfort her.
But look thou stay not till the watch be set,
For then thou canst not pass to Mantua,
Where thou shalt live till we can find a time
To blaze your marriage, reconcile your friends,
Beg pardon of the Prince, and call thee back
With twenty hundred thousand times more joy
Than thou went'st forth in lamentation.
Go before, nurse; commend me to thy lady;
And bid her hasten all the house to bed,
Which heavy sorrow makes them apt unto;
Romeo is coming.

Lines 119–134 omitted.

NURSE. O Lord, I could have stay'd here all the night
To hear good counsel; O, what learning is!
My lord, I'll tell my lady you will come.

ROM. Do so, and bid my sweet prepare to chide.

NURSE. Here, sir, a ring she bid me give you, sir.
Hie you, make haste, for it grows very late. [*Exit.*

ROM. How well my comfort is reviv'd by this!

FRI. L. Go hence; good night; and here stands all your state:
Either be gone before the watch be set,
Or by the break of day disguis'd from hence.
Sojourn in Mantua; I'll find out your man,
And he shall signify from time to time
Every good hap to you that chances here.
Give me thy hand. 'Tis late; farewell; good night.

ROM. But that a joy past joy calls out on me,
It were a grief so brief to part with thee.
Farewell. [*Exeunt.*

## SCENE IV. *Capulet's house.*

SCENE 19
*Interior. Capulet's House. The Hall. Night.*

*Enter* CAPULET, LADY CAPULET, *and* PARIS.

CAP. Things have fall'n out, sir, so unluckily
That we have had no time to move our daughter.
Look you, she lov'd her kinsman Tybalt dearly,
And so did I. Well, we were born to die.
'Tis very late; she'll not come down to-night.
I promise you, but for your company,
I would have been abed an hour ago.

PAR. These times of woe afford no time to woo.
Madam, good night; commend me to your daughter.
LADY C. I will, and know her mind early to-morrow;
To-night she's mew'd up to her heaviness.
CAP. Sir Paris, I will make a desperate tender
Of my child's love. I think she will be rul'd
In all respects by me; nay, more, I doubt it not.
Wife, go you to her ere you go to bed;
Acquaint her here of my son Paris' love
And bid her, mark you me, on Wednesday next—
But, soft! what day is this?
PAR. Monday, my lord.
CAP. Monday! ha, ha! Well, Wednesday is too soon.
A Thursday let it be; a Thursday, tell her,
She shall be married to this noble earl.
Will you be ready? Do you like this haste?
We'll keep no great ado—a friend or two;
For, hark you, Tybalt being slain so late,
It may be thought we held him carelessly,
Being our kinsman, if we revel much;
Therefore we'll have some half a dozen friends,
And there an end. But what say you to Thursday?
PAR. My lord, I would that Thursday were to-morrow.
CAP. Well, get you gone; a Thursday be it then.
Go you to Juliet ere you go to bed;
Prepare her, wife, against this wedding-day.
Farewell, my lord. Light to my chamber, ho!
Afore me, it is so very very late
That we may call it early by and by.
Good night. [*Exeunt.*

SCENE V. *Capulet's orchard.*

*Enter* ROMEO *and* JULIET, *aloft.*

SCENE 20
*Interior. Juliet's Bedroom. Night.*

JUL. Wilt thou be gone? It is not yet near day;
It was the nightingale, and not the lark,
That pierc'd the fearful hollow of thine ear;
Nightly she sings on yond pomegranate tree.
Believe me, love, it was the nightingale.
ROM. It was the lark, the herald of the morn,
No nightingale. Look, love, what envious streaks
Do lace the severing clouds in yonder east;
Night's candles are burnt out, and jocund day
Stands tiptoe on the misty mountain tops.
I must be gone and live, or stay and die.
JUL. Yond light is not daylight; I know it, I:
It is some meteor that the sun exhales
To be to thee this night a torch-bearer,
And light thee on thy way to Mantua;
Therefore stay yet; thou need'st not to be gone.
ROM. Let me be ta'en, let me be put to death;
I am content, so thou wilt have it so.
I'll say yon grey is not the morning's eye,
'Tis but the pale reflex of Cynthia's brow;

Nor that is not the lark whose notes do beat
The vaulty heaven so high above our heads.
I have more care to stay than will to go.
Come death, and welcome! Juliet wills it so.
How is't, my soul? Let's talk—it is not day.

JUL. It is, it is; hie hence, be gone, away!
It is the lark that sings so out of tune,
Straining harsh discords and unpleasing sharps.
Some say the lark makes sweet division;
This doth not so, for she divideth us.
Some say the lark and loathed toad change eyes
O, now I would they had chang'd voices too!
Since arm from arm that voice doth us affray,
Hunting thee hence with hunts-up to the day.
O, now be gone! More light and light it grows.

ROM. More light and light—more dark and dark our woes

*Enter* NURSE.

NURSE. Madam!

JUL. Nurse?

NURSE. Your lady mother is coming to your chamber.
The day is broke; be wary, look about. [*Exit.*

JUL. Then, window, let day in and let life out.

ROM. Farewell, farewell! One kiss, and I'll descend.
[*He goeth down.*

SCENE 21
*Exterior. Balcony. Early morning.*
ROMEO, JULIET

JUL. Art thou gone so, love—lord, ay, husband, friend!
I must hear from thee every day in the hour,
For in a minute there are many days;
O, by this count I shall be much in years
Ere I again behold my Romeo!

ROM. Farewell!
I will omit no opportunity
That may convey my greetings, love, to thee.

JUL. O, think'st thou we shall ever meet again?

ROM. I doubt it not; and all these woes shall serve
For sweet discourses in our times to come.

JUL. O God, I have an ill-divining soul!
Methinks I see thee, now thou art below,
As one dead in the bottom of a tomb;
Either my eyesight fails or thou look'st pale.

ROM. And trust me, love, in my eye so do you;
Dry sorrow drinks our blood. Adieu, adieu! [*Exit below.*

JUL. O Fortune, Fortune! all men call thee fickle.
If thou art fickle, what dost thou with him
That is renown'd for faith? Be fickle, Fortune;
For then, I hope, thou wilt not keep him long,
But send him back.

LADY C. [*Within.*] Ho, daughter! are you up?

SCENE 22
*Interior. Juliet's Bedroom. Early morning.*
LADY CAPULET, JULIET
Lines 65–67 omitted.

JUL. Who is't that calls? It is my lady mother.
Is she not down so late, or up so early?
What unaccustom'd cause procures her hither?

*Enter* LADY CAPULET.

LADY C. Why, how now, Juliet!

JUL. Madam, I am not well.
LADY C. Evermore weeping for your cousin's death?
What, wilt thou wash him from his grave with tears?
An if thou couldst, thou couldst not make him live;
Therefore have done. Some grief shows much of love
But much of grief shows still some want of wit.
JUL. Yet let me weep for such a feeling loss.
LADY C. So shall you feel the loss, but not the friend
Which you weep for.
JUL. Feeling so the loss,
I cannot choose but ever weep the friend.
LADY C. Well, girl, thou weep'st not so much for his death
As that the villain lives which slaughter'd him.
JUL. What villain, madam?
LADY C. That same villain, Romeo.
JUL. [*Aside.*] Villain and he be many miles asunder!—
God pardon him! I do, with all my heart;
And yet no man like he doth grieve my heart.
LADY C. That is because the traitor murderer lives.
JUL. Ay, madam, from the reach of these my hands.
Would none but I might venge my cousin's death!
LADY C. We will have vengeance for it, fear thou not;
Then weep no more. I'll send to one in Mantua—
Where that same banish'd runagate doth live—
Shall give him such an unaccustom'd dram
That he shall soon keep Tybalt company;
And then I hope thou wilt be satisfied.
JUL. Indeed I never shall be satisfied
With Romeo till I behold him—dead—
Is my poor heart so for a kinsman vex'd.
Line 95 omitted.
Madam, if you could find out but a man
To bear a poison, I would temper it,
That Romeo should, upon receipt thereof,
Soon sleep in quiet. O, how my heart abhors
To hear him nam'd, and cannot come to him,
To wreak the love I bore my cousin Tybalt
Upon his body that hath slaughter'd him!
Lines 101–102 omitted.
LADY C. Find thou the means, and I'll find such a man.
But now I'll tell thee joyful tidings, girl.
JUL. And joy comes well in such a needy time.
What are they, beseech your ladyship?
LADY C. Well, well, thou hast a careful father, child;
One who, to put thee from thy heaviness,
Hath sorted out a sudden day of joy
That thou expects not, nor I look'd not for.
JUL. Madam, in happy time, what day is that?
LADY C. Marry, my child, early next Thursday morn
The gallant, young, and noble gentleman,
The County Paris, at Saint Peter's Church,
Shall happily make thee there a joyful bride.
JUL. Now, by Saint Peter's Church, and Peter too,
He shall not make me there a joyful bride.
I wonder at this haste, that I must wed
Ere he that should be husband comes to woo.

I pray you tell my lord and father, madam,
I will not marry yet; and when I do, I swear
It shall be Romeo, whom you know I hate,
Rather than Paris. These are news indeed!

LADY C. Here comes your father; tell him so yourself,
And see how he will take it at your hands.

*Enter* CAPULET *and* NURSE.

CAP. When the sun sets, the air doth drizzle dew;
But for the sunset of my brother's son
It rains downright.
How now! a conduit, girl? What, still in tears?
Evermore show'ring? In one little body
Thou counterfeit'st a bark, a sea, a wind;
For still thy eyes, which I may call the sea,
Do ebb and flow with tears. The bark thy body is,
Sailing in this salt flood; the winds thy sighs,
Who, raging with thy tears, and they with them,
Without a sudden calm will overset
Thy tempest-tossed body. How now, wife!
Have you delivered to her our decree?

LADY C. Ay, sir; but she will none, she gives you thanks.
I would the fool were married to her grave!

CAP. Soft! take me with you, take me with you, wife.
How will she none? Doth she not give us thanks?
Is she not proud? Doth she not count her blest,
Unworthy as she is, that we have wrought
So worthy a gentleman to be her bridegroom?

JUL. Not proud you have, but thankful that you have.
Proud can I never be of what I hate,
But thankful even for hate that is meant love.

CAP. How how, how how, chopt logic! What is this?
'Proud'—and 'I thank you'—and 'I thank you not'—
And yet 'not proud'? Mistress minion, you,
Thank me no thankings, nor proud me no prouds,
But fettle your fine joints 'gainst Thursday next,
To go with Paris to Saint Peter's Church,
Or I will drag thee on a hurdle thither.
Out, you green-sickness carrion! Out, you baggage!
You tallow-face!

LADY C. Fie, fie! what, are you mad?

JUL. Good father, I beseech you on my knees,
Hear me with patience but to speak a word.

CAP. Hang thee, young baggage! disobedient wretch!
I tell thee what—get thee to church a Thursday,
Or never after look me in the face.
Speak not, reply not, do not answer me;
My fingers itch. Wife, we scarce thought us blest
That God had lent us but this only child;
But now I see this one is one too much,
And that we have a curse in having her.
Out on her, hilding!

NURSE. God in heaven bless her
You are to blame, my lord, to rate her so.

CAP. And why, my Lady Wisdom? Hold your tongue,
Good Prudence; smatter with your gossips, go.
NURSE. I speak no treason.
CAP. O, God-i-goden!
NURSE. May not one speak?
CAP. Peace, you mumbling fool!
Utter your gravity o'er a gossip's bowl,
For here we need it not.
LADY C. You are too hot.
CAP. God's bread! it makes me mad:
Day, night, hour, tide, time, work, play,
Alone, in company, still my care hath been
To have her match'd; and having now provided
A gentleman of noble parentage,
Of fair demesnes, youthful, and nobly train'd,
Stuff'd, as they say, with honourable parts,
Proportion'd as one's thought would wish a man—
And then to have a wretched puling fool,
A whining mammet, in her fortune's tender,
To answer 'I'll not wed, I cannot love,
I am too young, I pray you pardon me'!
But, an you will not wed, I'll pardon you.
Graze where you will, you shall not house with me.
Look to't, think on't; I do not use to jest.
Thursday is near; lay hand on heart advise:
An you be mine, I'll give you to my friend;
An you be not, hang, beg, starve, die in the streets,
For, by my soul, I'll ne'er acknowledge thee,
Nor what is mine shall never do thee good.
Trust to't, bethink you, I'll not be forsworn. [*Exit.*
JUL. Is there no pity sitting in the clouds
That sees into the bottom of my grief?
O, sweet my mother, cast me not away!
Delay this marriage for a month, a week;
Or, if you do not, make the bridal bed
In that dim monument where Tybalt lies.
LADY C. Talk not to me, for I'll not speak a word;
Do as thou wilt, for I have done with thee. [*Exit.*
JUL. O God!—O nurse! how shall this be prevented?
My husband is on earth, my faith in heaven;
How shall that faith return again to earth,
Unless that husband send it me from heaven
By leaving earth? Comfort me, counsel me.
Alack, alack, that heaven should practise stratagems
Upon so soft a subject as myself!
What say'st thou! Hast thou not a word of joy?
Some comfort, nurse.
NURSE. Faith, here it is:
Romeo is banished; and all the world to nothing
That he dares ne'er come back to challenge you;
Or, if he do, it needs must be by stealth.
Then, since the case so stands as now it doth,
I think it best you married with the County.
O, he's a lovely gentleman!

Romeo's a dishclout to him ; an eagle, madam,
Hath not so green, so quick, so fair an eye
As Paris hath. Beshrew my very heart,
I think you are happy in this second match,
For it excels your first ; or, if it did not,
Your first is dead, or 'twere as good he were
As living here and you no use of him.

JUL. Speak'st thou from thy heart ?

NURSE. And from my soul too, else beshrew them both.

JUL. Amen !

NURSE. What ?

JUL. Well, thou hast comforted me marvellous much.
Go in ; and tell my lady I am gone,
Having displeas'd my father, to Lawrence' cell
To make confession, and to be absolv'd.

NURSE. Marry, I will ; and this is wisely done. [*Exit.*

JUL. Ancient damnation ! O most wicked fiend !
Is it more sin to wish me thus forsworn,
Or to dispraise my lord with that same tongue
Which she hath prais'd him with above compare
So many thousand times ? Go, counsellor ;
Thou and my bosom henceforth shall be twain.
I'll to the friar to know his remedy ;
If all else fail, myself have power to die. [*Exit.*

## ACT FOUR

### SCENE I. *Friar Lawrence's cell.*

SCENE 23
*Exterior. The Cloisters. Day.*

*Enter* FRIAR LAWRENCE *and* COUNTY PARIS.

FRI. L. On Thursday, sir ? The time is very short.

PAR. My father Capulet will have it so,
And I am nothing slow to slack his haste.

FRI. L. You say you do not know the lady's mind ;
Uneven is the course ; I like it not.

PAR. Immoderately she weeps for Tybalt's death,
And therefore have I little talk'd of love ;
For Venus smiles not in a house of tears.
Now, sir, her father counts it dangerous
That she do give her sorrow so much sway,
And in his wisdom hastes our marriage,
To stop the inundation of her tears ;
Which, too much minded by herself alone,
May be put from her by society.
Now do you know the reason of this haste.

FRI. L. [*Aside.*] I would I knew not why it should be slow'd.—
Look, sir, here comes the lady toward my cell.

*Enter* JULIET.

PAR. Happily met, my lady and my wife !

JUL. That may be, sir, when I may be a wife.

PAR. That may be must be, love, on Thursday next.

JUL. What must be shall be.

FRI. L. That's a certain text.
PAR. Come you to make confession to this father?
JUL. To answer that, I should confess to you.
PAR. Do not deny to him that you love me.
JUL. I will confess to you that I love him.
PAR. So will ye, I am sure, that you love me.
JUL. If I do so, it will be of more price
Being spoke behind your back than to your face.
PAR. Poor soul, thy face is much abus'd with tears.
JUL. The tears have got small victory by that,
For it was bad enough before their spite.
PAR. Thou wrong'st it more than tears with that report.
JUL. That is no slander, sir, which is a truth;
And what I spake, I spake it to my face.
PAR. Thy face is mine, and thou hast sland'red it.
JUL. It may be so, for it is not mine own.
Are you at leisure, holy father, now,
Or shall I come to you at evening mass?
FRI. L. My leisure serves me, pensive daughter, now.
My lord, we must entreat the time alone.
PAR. God shield I should disturb devotion!
Juliet, on Thursday early will I rouse ye;
Till then, adieu, and keep this holy kiss. *Exit.*
JUL. O, shut the door, and when thou hast done so,
Come weep with me—past hope, past cure, past help.
FRI. L. O, Juliet, I already know thy grief;
It strains me past the compass of my wits.
I hear thou must, and nothing may prorogue it,
On Thursday next be married to this County.
JUL. Tell me not, friar, that thou hear'st of this,
Unless thou tell me how I may prevent it;
If, in thy wisdom, thou canst give no help,
Do thou but call my resolution wise,
And with this knife I'll help it presently.
God join'd my heart and Romeo's, thou our hands;
And ere this hand, by thee to Romeo's seal'd,
Shall be the label to another deed,
Or my true heart with treacherous revolt
Turn to another, this shall slay them both.
Therefore, out of thy long-experienc'd time,
Give me some present counsel; or, behold,
'Twixt my extremes and me this bloody knife
Shall play the umpire, arbitrating that
Which the commission of thy years and art
Could to no issue of true honour bring.
Be not so long to speak; I long to die,
If what thou speak'st speak not of remedy.
FRI. L. Hold, daughter; I do spy a kind of hope,
Which craves as desperate an execution
As that is desperate which we would prevent.
If, rather than to marry County Paris,
Thou hast the strength of will to slay thyself,
Then is it likely thou wilt undertake
A thing like death to chide away this shame,

Lines 29–36 omitted.

SCENE 24
*Interior. Friar Lawrence's Cell. Day.*
JULIET, FRIAR LAWRENCE

That cop'st with death himself to scape from it;
And, if thou dar'st, I'll give thee remedy.

Lines 75–76 omitted.

JUL. O, bid me leap, rather than marry Paris,
From off the battlements of any tower,
Or walk in thievish ways, or bid me lurk
Where serpents are; chain me with roaring bears,
Or hide me nightly in a charnel house,
O'er-cover'd quite with dead men's rattling bones,
With reeky shanks and yellow chapless skulls;
Or bid me go into a new-made grave,
And hide me with a dead man in his shroud—
Things that, to hear them told, have made me tremble—
And I will do it without fear or doubt,
To live an unstain'd wife to my sweet love.

FRI. L. Hold, then; go home, be merry, give consent
To marry Paris. Wednesday is to-morrow;
To-morrow night look that thou lie alone,
Let not the nurse lie with thee in thy chamber.
Take thou this vial, being then in bed,
And this distilled liquor drink thou off;
When presently through all thy veins shall run
A cold and drowsy humour; for no pulse
Shall keep his native progress, but surcease;
No warmth, no breath, shall testify thou livest;
The roses in thy lips and cheeks shall fade
To paly ashes, thy eyes' windows fall,
Like death when he shuts up the day of life;
Each part, depriv'd of supple government,
Shall, stiff and stark and cold, appear like death;
And in this borrow'd likeness of shrunk death
Thou shalt continue two and forty hours,
And then awake as from a pleasant sleep.
Now, when the bridegroom in the morning comes
To rouse thee from thy bed, there art thou dead.
Then, as the manner of our country is,
In thy best robes, uncovered on the bier,
Thou shalt be borne to that same ancient vault
Where all the kindred of the Capulets lie.
In the meantime, against thou shalt awake,
Shall Romeo by my letters know our drift,
And hither shall he come; and he and I
Will watch thy waking, and that very night
Shall Romeo bear thee hence to Mantua.
And this shall free thee from this present shame,
If no inconstant toy nor womanish fear
Abate thy valour in the acting it.

'against thou shalt awake' omitted.

JUL. Give me, give me! O, tell not me of fear!

FRI. L. Hold; get you gone, be strong and prosperous
In this resolve. I'll send a friar with speed
To Mantua, with my letters to thy lord.

JUL. Love give me strength! and strength shall help afford.
Farewell, dear father! [*Exeunt.*

SCENE II. *Capulet's house.*

*Enter* CAPULET, LADY CAPULET, NURSE, *and two or three* SERVINGMEN.

CAP. So many guests invite as here are writ. [*Exit a* SERVINGMAN.
Sirrah, go hire me twenty cunning cooks.

SERV. You shall have none ill, sir; for I'll try if they can lick their fingers.

CAP. How canst thou try them so?

SERV. Marry, sir, 'tis an ill cook that cannot lick his own fingers; therefore he that cannot lick his fingers goes not with me.

CAP. Go, be gone. [*Exit second* SERVINGMAN.
We shall be much unfurnish'd for this time.
What, is my daughter gone to Friar Lawrence?

NURSE. Ay, forsooth.

CAP. Well, he may chance to do some good on her:
A peevish self-will'd harlotry it is.

*Enter* JULIET.

NURSE. See where she comes from shrift with merry look.

CAP. How now, my headstrong! Where have you been gadding?

JUL. Where I have learnt me to repent the sin
Of disobedient opposition
To you and your behests; and am enioin'd
By holy Lawrence to fall prostrate here,
To beg your pardon. Pardon, I beseech you.
Henceforward I am ever rul'd by you.

CAP. Send for the County; go tell him of this.
I'll have this knot knit up to-morrow morning.

JUL. I met the youthful lord at Lawrence' cell,
And gave him what becomed love I might,
Not stepping o'er the bounds of modesty.

CAP. Why, I am glad on't; this is well—stand up—
This is as't should be. Let me see the County;
Ay, marry, go, I say, and fetch him hither.
Now, afore God, this reverend holy friar,
All our whole city is much bound to him.

JUL. Nurse, will you go with me into my closet
To help me sort such needful ornaments
As you think fit to furnish me to-morrow?

LADY C. No, not till Thursday; there is time enough.

CAP. Go, nurse, go with her. We'll to church to-morrow.
[*Exeunt* JULIET *and* NURSE.

LADY C. We shall be short in our provision;
'Tis now near night.

CAP. Tush, I will stir about,
And all things shall be well, I warrant thee, wife.
Go thou to Juliet, help to deck up her;
I'll not to bed to-night; let me alone.
I'll play the huswife for this once. What, ho!
They are all forth; well, I will walk myself
To County Paris, to prepare up him
Against to-morrow. My heart is wondrous light
Since this same wayward girl is so reclaim'd. [*Exeunt.*

SCENE 25
*Exterior. Capulet's Orchard. Day.*

Lines 1–14 omitted.

*Enter* SAMSON *and* PETER

SAM. Thou art a poltroon.

PET. Samson.

SAM. Anon.

PET. My fan. Before and apace.

JULIET *enters the house.*

SCENE 26
*Interior. Capulet's House. The Hall. Day.*

CAPULET, LADY CAPULET, JULIET, NURSE

Line 15 omitted.

SCENE III. *Juliet's chamber.*

SCENE 27
*Interior. Juliet's Bedroom. Night.*

*Enter* JULIET *and* NURSE.

JUL. Ay, those attires are best; but, gentle nurse,
I pray thee, leave me to myself to-night,
For I have need of many orisons
To move the heavens to smile upon my state,
Which well thou knowest is cross and full of sin.

*Enter* LADY CAPULET.

LADY C. What, are you busy, ho? Need you my help?
JUL. No, madam; we have cull'd such necessaries
As are behoveful for our state to-morrow.
So please you, let me now be left alone,
And let the nurse this night sit up with you;
For I am sure you have your hands full all
In this so sudden business.
LADY C. Good night.
Get thee to bed, and rest; for thou hast need.
[*Exeunt* LADY CAPULET *and* NURSE.
JUL. Farewell! God knows when we shall meet again.
I have a faint cold fear thrills through my veins,
That almost freezes up the heat of life;
I'll call them back again to comfort me.
Nurse!—What should she do here?
My dismal scene I needs must act alone.
Come, vial.
What if this mixture do not work at all?
Shall I be married, then, to-morrow morning?
No, no; this shall forbid it. Lie thou there.
[*Laying down her dagger.*
What if it be a poison which the friar
Subtly hath minist'red to have me dead,
Lest in this marriage he should be dishonour'd,
Because he married me before to Romeo?
I fear it is; and yet methinks it should not,
For he hath still been tried a holy man.
How, if, when I am laid into the tomb,
I wake before the time that Romeo
Come to redeem me? There's a fearful point.
Shall I not then be stifled in the vault,
To whose foul mouth no healthsome air breathes in,
And there die strangled ere my Romeo comes?
Or, if I live, is it not very like
The horrible conceit of death and night,
Together with the terror of the place—
As in a vault, an ancient receptacle
Where for this many hundred years the bones
Of all my buried ancestors are pack'd;
Where bloody Tybalt, yet but green in earth,
Lies fest'ring in his shroud; where, as they say,
At some hours in the night spirits resort—
Alack, alack, is it not like that I,

So early waking—what with loathsome smells,
And shrieks like mandrakes' torn out of the earth,
That living mortals, hearing them, run mad—
O, if I wake, shall I not be distraught,
Environed with all these hideous fears,
And madly play with my forefathers' joints,
And pluck the mangled Tybalt from his shroud,
And, in this rage, with some great kinsman's bone,
As with a club, dash out my desp'rate brains?
O, look! methinks I see my cousin's ghost
Seeking out Romeo, that did spit his body
Upon a rapier's point. Stay, Tybalt, stay.
Romeo, I come. This do I drink to thee.
[*She drinks and falls upon her bed within the curtains.*

SCENE IV. *Capulet's house.*

SCENE 28
*Interior. Capulet's House. Scullery. Night.*

*Enter* LADY CAPULET *and* NURSE.

LADY C. Hold, take these keys, and fetch more spices, nurse.
NURSE. They call for dates and quinces in the pastry.

*Enter* CAPULET.

CAP. Come, stir, stir, stir! The second cock hath crow'd,
The curfew bell hath rung, 'tis three o'clock.
Look to the bak'd meats, good Angelica;
Spare not for cost.
NURSE. Go, you cot-quean, go,
Get you to bed; faith, you'll be sick to-morrow
For this night's watching.
CAP. No, not a whit; what! I have watch'd ere now
All night for lesser cause, and ne'er been sick.
LADY C. Ay, you have been a mouse-hunt in your time;
But I will watch you from such watching now.
[*Exeunt* LADY CAPULET *and* NURSE.
CAP. A jealous-hood, a jealous-hood!

*Enter three or four* SERVINGMEN *with spits and logs and baskets.*

Now, fellow,
What is there?
1 FELLOW. Things for the cook, sir; but I know not what.
CAP. Make haste, make haste. [*Exit* 1 FELLOW.
Sirrah, fetch drier logs;
Call Peter; he will show thee where they are.
2 FELLOW. I have a head, sir, that will find out logs,
And never trouble Peter for the matter.
CAP. Mass, and well said; a merry whoreson, ha!
Thou shalt be logger-head. [*Exit* 2 FELLOW.
Good faith, 'tis day;
The County will be here with music straight,
For so he said he would. [*Play music.*] I hear him near.
Nurse! Wife! What, ho! What, nurse, I say!

*Re-enter* NURSE.

Go waken Juliet, go and trim her up;

I'll go and chat with Paris. Hie, make haste,
Make haste. The bridegroom he is come already.
Make haste, I say. [*Exeunt.*

SCENE V. *Juliet's chamber.*

SCENE 29
*Interior. Juliet's Bedroom. Day.*

*Enter* Nurse.

NURSE. Mistress! What, mistress! Juliet! Fast, I warrant her, she.
Why, lamb! Why, lady! Fie, you slug-a-bed!
Why, love, I say! madam! sweetheart! Why, bride!
What, not a word? You take your pennyworths now.
Sleep for a week; for the next night, I warrant,
The County Paris hath set up his rest
That you shall rest but little. God forgive me!
Marry, and amen. How sound is she asleep!
I needs must wake her. Madam, madam, madam!
Ay, let the County take you in your bed;
He'll fright you up, i' faith. Will it not be? [*Draws the curtains.*
What, dress'd, and in your clothes, and down again!
I must needs wake you. Lady! lady! lady!
Alas, alas! Help, help! my lady's dead!
O well-a-day that ever I was born!
Some aqua-vitæ, ho! My lord! My lady!

*Enter* LADY CAPULET.

LADY C. What noise is here?
NURSE. O lamentable day!
LADY C. What is the matter?
NURSE. Look, look! O heavy day!
LADY C. O me, O me! My child, my only life,
Revive, look up, or I will die with thee!
Help, help! Call help.

*Enter* CAPULET.

CAP. For shame, bring Juliet forth; her lord is come.
NURSE. She's dead, deceas'd, she's dead; alack the day!
LADY C. Alack the day, she's dead, she's dead, she's dead!
CAP. Ha! let me see her. Out, alas! she's cold;
Her blood is settled, and her joints are stiff.
Life and these lips have long been separated.
Death lies on her like an untimely frost
Upon the sweetest flower of all the field.
NURSE. O lamentable day!
LADY C. O woeful time!
CAP. Death, that hath ta'en her hence to make me wail,
Ties up my tongue and will not let me speak.

*Enter* FRIAR LAWRENCE *and* COUNTY PARIS, *with* MUSICIANS.

FRI. L. Come, is the bride ready to go to church?
CAP. Ready to go, but never to return.
O son, the night before thy wedding day
Hath Death lain with thy wife. There she lies,

Flower as she was, deflowered by him.
Death is my son-in-law, Death is my heir;
My daughter he hath wedded; I will die,
And leave him all; life, living, all is Death's.

PAR. Have I thought long to see this morning's face,
And doth it give me such a sight as this?

LADY C. Accurs'd, unhappy, wretched, hateful day!
Most miserable hour that e'er time saw
In lasting labour of his pilgrimage!
But one, poor one, one poor and loving child,
But one thing to rejoice and solace in,
And cruel Death hath catch'd it from my sight!

NURSE. O woe! O woeful, woeful, woeful day!
Most lamentable day, most woeful day
That ever, ever, I did yet behold!
O day! O day! O day! O hateful day!
Never was seen so black a day as this.
O woeful day, O woeful day!

Lines 53–59 omitted.

PAR. Beguil'd, divorced, wronged, spited, slain!
Most detestable Death, by thee beguil'd,
By cruel cruel thee quite overthrown!
O love! O life!—not life, but love in death!

CAP. Despis'd, distressed, hated, martyr'd, kill'd!—
Uncomfortable time, why cam'st thou now
To murder, murder our solemnity?
O child! O child! my soul, and not my child!
Dead art thou; alack, my child is dead,
And with my child my joys are buried.

FRI. L. Peace, ho, for shame! Confusion's cure lives not
In these confusions. Heaven and yourself
Had part in this fair maid; now heaven hath all,
And all the better is it for the maid.
Your part in her you could not keep from death,
But heaven keeps his part in eternal life.
The most you sought was her promotion,
For 'twas your heaven she should be advanc'd
And weep ye now, seeing she is advanc'd
Above the clouds, as high as heaven itself?
O, in this love, you love your child so ill
That you run mad, seeing that she is well.
She's not well married that lives married long,
But she's best married that dies married young.
Dry up your tears, and stick your rosemary
On this fair corse, and, as the custom is,
In all her best array bear her to church;
For though fond nature bids us all lament,
Yet nature's tears are reason's merriment.

Lines 69–78 omitted.

CAP. All things that we ordained festival
Turn from their office to black funeral:
Our instruments to melancholy bells,
Our wedding cheer to a sad burial feast,
Our solemn hymns to sullen dirges change;
Our bridal flowers serve for a buried corse;
And all things change them to the contrary.

FRI. L. Sir, go you in; and, madam, go with him;
And go, Sir Paris. Every one prepare
To follow this fair corse unto her grave.
The heavens do lour upon you for some ill;
Move them no more by crossing their high will.
[*Exeunt all but* NURSE *and* MUSICIANS.

SCENE 30
*Interior. Capulet's House. The Hall. Day.*
PETER, MUSICIANS
Lines 97–99 omitted.

1 MUS. Faith, we may put up our pipes and be gone.
NURSE. Honest good fellows, ah, put up, put up;
For well you know this is a pitiful case. [*Exit.*
1 MUS. Ay, by my troth, the case may be amended.

*Enter* PETER.

PET. Musicians, O, musicians, 'Heart's ease,' 'Heart's ease!' O, an you will have me live, play 'Heart's ease.'
1 MUS. Why 'Heart's ease?'
PET. O, musicians, because my heart itself plays 'My heart is full of woe.' O, play me some merry dump to comfort me.
1 MUS. Not a dump we! 'Tis no time to play now.

'You will not, then' to end of scene omitted.

PET. You will not, then?
1 MUS. No.
PET. I will then give it you soundly.
1 MUS. What will you give us?
PET. No money, on my faith, but the gleek. I will give you the minstrel.
1 MUS. Then I will give you the serving-creature.
PET. Then will I lay the serving-creature's dagger on your pate. I will carry no crotchets: I'll re you, I'll fa you; do you note me?
1 MUS. An you re us and fa us, you note us.
2 MUS. Pray you put up your dagger, and put out your wit.
PET. Then have at you with my wit! I will dry-beat you with an iron wit, and put up my iron dagger. Answer me like men.

'When griping grief the heart doth wound
And doleful dumps the mind oppress,
Then music with her silver sound'—

Why 'silver sound'? Why 'music with her silver sound'? What say you, Simon Catling?
1 MUS. Marry, sir, because silver hath a sweet sound.
PET. Pretty! What say you, Hugh Rebeck?
2 MUS. I say 'silver sound' because musicians sound for silver.
PET. Pretty too! What say you, James Soundpost?
3 MUS. Faith, I know not what to say.
PET. O, I cry you mercy, you are the singer; I will say for you. It is 'music with her silver sound' because musicians have no gold for sounding.
'Then music with her silver sound
With speedy help doth lend redress.' [*Exit.*
1 MUS. What a pestilent knave is this same!
2 MUS. Hang him, Jack! Come, we'll in here; tarry for the mourners, and stay dinner. [*Exeunt.*

## ACT FIVE

SCENE I. *Mantua. A street.*

*Enter* ROMEO.

SCENE 31
*Exterior. Mantua.*
*A Street. Day.*

ROM. If I may trust the flattering truth of sleep,
My dreams presage some joyful news at hand.
My bosom's lord sits lightly in his throne,
And all this day an unaccustom'd spirit
Lifts me above the ground with cheerful thoughts.
I dreamt my lady came and found me dead—
Strange dream, that gives a dead man leave to think !—
And breath'd such life with kisses in my lips
That I reviv'd, and was an emperor.
Ah me ! how sweet is love itself possess'd,
When but love's shadows are so rich in joy !

Lines 10–11 omitted.

*Enter* BALTHASAR, *Romeo's man.*

News from Verona ! How now, Balthasar !
Dost thou not bring me letters from the friar ?
How doth my lady ? Is my father well ?
How fares my Juliet ? That I ask again,
For nothing can be ill if she be well.
BAL. Then she is well, and nothing can be ill.
Her body sleeps in Capels' monument,
And her immortal part with angels lives.
I saw her laid low in her kindred's vault,
And presently took post to tell it you.
O, pardon me for bringing these ill news,
Since you did leave it for my office, sir.
ROM. Is it e'en so ? Then I defy you, stars.
Thou knowest my lodging : get me ink and paper,
And hire post-horses ; I will hence to-night.
BAL. I do beseech you, sir, have patience ;
Your looks are pale and wild, and do import
Some misadventure.
ROM. Tush, thou art deceiv'd ;
Leave me, and do the thing I bid thee do.
Hast thou no letters to me from the friar ?
BAL. No, my good lord.
ROM. No matter ; get thee gone,
And hire those horses ; I'll be with thee straight.
[*Exit* BALTHASAR.

Lines 24–25, from 'Then I defy you', omitted.
Line 26, for 'And' read 'Go'.

Line 33 omitted.

Well, Juliet, I will lie with thee to-night.
Let's see for means. O mischief, thou art swift
To enter in the thoughts of desperate men !
I do remember an apothecary,
And hereabouts 'a dwells, which late I noted
In tatt'red weeds, with overwhelming brows,
Culling of simples. Meagre were his looks ;
Sharp misery had worn him to the bones ;
And in his needy shop a tortoise hung,
An alligator stuff'd, and other skins

Lines 36–56 omitted.

Lines 36–56 omitted.

Of ill-shap'd fishes; and about his shelves
A beggarly account of empty boxes,
Green earthen pots, bladders, and musty seeds,
Remnants of packthread, and old cakes of roses,
Were thinly scattered, to make up a show.
Noting this penury, to myself I said
'An if a man did need a poison now,
Whose sale is present death in Mantua,
Here lives a caitiff wretch would sell it him.'
O, this same thought did but forerun my need
And this same needy man must sell it me.
As I remember, this should be the house.
Being holiday, the beggar's shop is shut.
What, ho! Apothecary!

*Enter* APOTHECARY.

SCENE 32
*Interior. Mantua.*
*Apothecary's Shop.*
*Day.*

AP. Who calls so loud?
ROM. Come hither, man. I see that thou art poor.
Hold, there is forty ducats; let me have
A dram of poison, such soon-speeding gear
As will disperse itself through all the veins
That the life-weary taker may fall dead,
And that the trunk may be discharg'd of breath
As violently as hasty powder fir'd
Doth hurry from the fatal cannon's womb.

Lines 63–65 omitted.

AP. Such mortal drugs I have; but Mantua's law
Is death to any he that utters them.
ROM. Art thou so bare and full of wretchedness
And fearest to die? Famine is in thy cheeks,
Need and oppression starveth in thy eyes,
Contempt and beggary hangs upon thy back,
The world is not thy friend, nor the world's law;
The world affords no law to make thee rich;
Then be not poor, but break it and take this.
AP. My poverty but not my will consents.
ROM. I pay thy poverty and not thy will.
AP. Put this in any liquid thing you will
And drink it off; and if you had the strength
Of twenty men, it would dispatch you straight.
ROM. There is thy gold—worse poison to men's souls,
Doing more murder in this loathsome world
Than these poor compounds that thou mayst not sell.
I sell thee poison: thou hast sold me none.
Farewell; buy food, and get thyself in flesh.
Come, cordial and not poison, go with me
To Juliet's grave; for there must I use thee. [*Exeunt.*

Lines 84–86 omitted.

SCENE II. *Friar Lawrence's cell.*

*Enter* FRIAR JOHN.

SCENE 33
*Exterior. Verona.*
*The Cloisters. Day.*

FRI. J. Holy Franciscan friar! Brother, ho!

*Enter* FRIAR LAWRENCE.

FRI. L. This same should be the voice of Friar John.

Line 2 omitted.

Welcome from Mantua! What says Romeo?
Or, if his mind be writ, give me his letter.

FRI. J. Going to find a barefoot brother out,
One of our order, to associate me,
Here in this city visiting the sick,
And finding him, the searchers of the town,
Suspecting that we both were in a house
Where the infectious pestilence did reign,
Seal'd up the doors, and would not let us forth,
So that my speed to Mantua there was stay'd.

FRI. L. Who bare my letter, then, to Romeo?

FRI. J. I could not send it—here it is again—
Nor get a messenger to bring it thee,
So fearful were they of infection.

FRI. L. Unhappy fortune! By my brotherhood,
The letter was not nice, but full of charge
Of dear import; and the neglecting it
May do much danger. Friar John, go hence;
Get me an iron crow, and bring it straight
Unto my cell.

FRI. J. Brother, I'll go and bring it thee. [*Exit.*

FRI. L. Now must I to the monument alone.
Within this three hours will fair Juliet wake;
She will beshrew me much that Romeo
Hath had not notice of these accidents.
But I will write again to Mantua,
And keep her at my cell till Romeo come—
Poor living corse, clos'd in a dead man's tomb! [*Exit.*

SCENE III. *Verona. A churchyard; in it the tomb of the Capulets.*

SCENE 34
*Exterior. Verona. Churchyard. Night.*

*Enter* PARIS, *and his* PAGE *bearing flowers and a torch.*

PAR. Give me thy torch, boy; hence, and stand aloof;
Yet put it out, for I would not be seen.
Under yond yew trees lay thee all along,
Holding thy ear close to the hollow ground;
So shall no foot upon the churchyard tread—
Being loose, unfirm, with digging up of graves—
But thou shalt hear it. Whistle then to me,
As signal that thou hearest something approach.
Give me those flowers. Do as I bid thee, go.

Lines 2–11 omitted.

PAGE. [*Aside.*] I am almost afraid to stand alone
Here in the churchyard; yet I will adventure. [*Retires.*

PAR. Sweet flower, with flowers thy bridal bed I strew—
O woe, thy canopy is dust and stones!—
Which with sweet water nightly I will dew;
Or, wanting that, with tears distill'd by moans.
The obsequies that I for thee will keep,
Nightly shall be to strew thy grave and weep.
[*The* PAGE *whistles.*
The boy gives warning something doth approach.
What cursed foot wanders this way to-night

To cross my obsequies and true love's rite?
What, with a torch! Muffle me, night, awhile. [*Retires.*

*Enter* ROMEO *and* BALTHASAR, *with a torch, a mattock, and a crow of iron.*

ROM. Give me that mattock and the wrenching iron.
Hold, take this letter; early in the morning
See thou deliver it to my lord and father.
Give me the light; upon thy life I charge thee,
Whate'er thou hearest or seest, stand all aloof
And do not interrupt me in my course.
Why I descend into this bed of death
Is partly to behold my lady's face,
But chiefly to take thence from her dead finger
A precious ring—a ring that I must use
In dear employment; therefore hence, be gone.
But if thou, jealous, dost return to pry
In what I farther shall intend to do,
By heaven, I will tear thee joint by joint,
And strew this hungry churchyard with thy limbs.
The time and my intents are savage-wild,
More fierce and more inexorable far
Than empty tigers or the roaring sea.

Lines 22–24 omitted.

Lines 28–32 omitted.

BAL. I will be gone, sir, and not trouble ye.
ROM. So shalt thou show me friendship.
Take thou that;
Live and be prosperous; and farewell, good fellow.
BAL. [*Aside.*] For all this same, I'll hide me hereabout;
His looks I fear, and his intents I doubt. [*Retires.*
ROM. Thou detestable maw, thou womb of death,
Gorg'd with the dearest morsel of the earth,
Thus I enforce thy rotten jaws to open, [*Breaking open the tomb.*
And, in despite, I'll cram thee with more food.
PAR. This is that banish'd haughty Montague
That murd'red my love's cousin—with which grief
It is supposed the fair creature died—
And here is come to do some villainous shame
To the dead bodies. I will apprehend him.
Stop thy unhallowed toil, vile Montague.
Can vengeance be pursued further than death?
Condemned villain, I do apprehend thee.
Obey, and go with me; for thou must die.
ROM. I must indeed; and therefore came I hither.
Good gentle youth, tempt not a desp'rate man;
Fly hence, and leave me. Think upon these gone;
Let them affright thee. I beseech thee, youth,
Put not another sin upon my head
By urging me to fury; O, be gone!
By heaven, I love thee better than myself,
For I come hither arm'd against myself.
Stay not, be gone; live, and hereafter say
A madman's mercy bid thee run away.
PAR. I do defy thy conjuration,
And apprehend thee for a felon here.
ROM. Wilt thou provoke me? Then have at thee, boy! [*They fight.*

Lines 60–61 omitted.

| PAGE. O lord, they fight! I will go call the watch.
[*Exit.* PARIS *falls.*

PAR. O, I am slain! If thou be merciful,
Open the tomb, lay me with Juliet. [*Dies.*

ROM. In faith, I will. Let me peruse this face.
Mercutio's kinsman, noble County Paris!
What said my man, when my betossed soul
Did not attend him as we rode? I think
He told me Paris should have married Juliet.
Said he not so, or did I dream it so?
Or am I mad, hearing him talk of Juliet,
To think it was so? O, give me thy hand,
One writ with me in sour misfortune's book!
I'll bury thee in a triumphant grave.
A grave? O no! A lantern, slaught'red youth;
For here lies Juliet, and her beauty makes
This vault a feasting presence full of light.
| Death, lie thou there, by a dead man interr'd.
[*Laying* PARIS *in the tomb.*
| How oft when men are at the point of death
| Have they been merry! Which their keepers call
| A lightning before death. O, how may I
| Call this a lightning? O my love! my wife!
Death, that hath suck'd the honey of thy breath,
Hath had no power yet upon thy beauty.
Thou art not conquer'd; beauty's ensign yet
Is crimson in thy lips and in thy cheeks,
And death's pale flag is not advanced there.
Tybalt, liest thou there in thy bloody sheet?
O, what more favour can I do to thee
Than with that hand that cut thy youth in twain
To sunder his that was thine enemy?
Forgive me, cousin. Ah, dear Juliet,
Why art thou yet so fair? Shall I believe
That unsubstantial Death is amorous,
And that the lean abhorred monster keeps
Thee here in dark to be his paramour?
For fear of that I still will stay with thee,
And never from this palace of dim night
Depart again. Here, here will I remain
With worms that are thy chambermaids. O, here
Will I set up my everlasting rest,
And shake the yoke of inauspicious stars
From this world-wearied flesh. Eyes, look your last.
Arms, take your last embrace. And, lips, O you
The doors of breath, seal with a righteous kiss
A dateless bargain to engrossing death!
Come, bitter conduct, come, unsavoury guide.
| Thou desperate pilot, now at once run on
| The dashing rocks thy sea-sick weary bark.
Here's to my love! [*Drinks.*] O true apothecary!
Thy drugs are quick. Thus with a kiss I die. [*Falls.*

*Enter* FRIAR LAWRENCE, *with lantern, crow, and spade.*

| 'O lord, they fight' omitted. Rest of line and PAGE's exit take place after line 83.

PAGE. I will go call the watch. [*Exit*]
SCENE 35
*Interior. Verona.*
*The Capulets' Tomb.*
| *Night.*
ROMEO
| Lines 87–91, to 'Call this a lightning', omitted.

| Lines 117–118 omitted.

SCENE 36
*Exterior. Verona.*
*Churchyard. Night.*

FRI. L. Saint Francis be my speed! How oft to-night
Have my old feet stumbled at graves! Who's there?
BAL. Here's one, a friend, and one that knows you well.
FRI. L. Bliss be upon you! Tell me, good my friend,
What torch is yond that vainly lends his light
To grubs and eyeless skulls? As I discern,
It burneth in the Capels' monument.
BAL. It doth so, holy sir; and there's my master,
One that you love.
FRI. L. Who is it?
BAL. Romeo.
FRI. L. How long hath he been there?
BAL. Full half an hour.
FRI. L. Go with me to the vault.
BAL. I dare not, sir.
My master knows not but I am gone hence,
And fearfully did menace me with death,
If I did stay to look on his intents.
FRI. L. Stay, then, I'll go alone; fear comes upon me;
O, much I fear some ill unthrifty thing.
BAL. As I did sleep under this yew tree here,
I dreamt my master and another fought,
And that my master slew him.
FRI. L. Romeo!

Lines 137–139 omitted.

Alack, alack, what blood is this which stains
The stony entrance of this sepulchre?
What mean these masterless and gory swords
To lie discolour'd by this place of peace? [*Enters the tomb.*

SCENE 37
*Interior. Verona. The Capulets' Tomb. Night.*
FRIAR LAWRENCE, JULIET
After line 150, add:
I WATCH. [*within.*] Lead, boy. Which way?

Romeo! O, pale! Who else? What, Paris too?
And steep'd in blood? Ah, what an unkind hour
Is guilty of this lamentable chance!
The lady stirs. [JULIET *wakes.*
JUL. O comfortable friar! Where is my lord?
I do remember well where I should be,
And there I am. Where is my Romeo? [*Noise within.*
FRI. L. I hear some noise. Lady, come from that nest
Of death, contagion, and unnatural sleep;
A greater power than we can contradict
Hath thwarted our intents. Come, come away;
Thy husband in thy bosom there lies dead;
And Paris too. Come, I'll dispose of thee
Among a sisterhood of holy nuns.
Stay not to question, for the watch is coming;
Come, go, good Juliet. I dare no longer stay.
JUL. Go, get thee hence, for I will not away. [*Exit* FRIAR LAWRENCE.
What's here? A cup, clos'd in my true love's hand?
Poison, I see, hath been his timeless end.
O churl! drunk all, and left no friendly drop
To help me after? I will kiss thy lips;
Haply some poison yet doth hang on them,
To make me die with a restorative. [*Kisses him.*
Thy lips are warm.
I WATCH. [*Within.*] Lead, boy. Which way?

Transposed above.
Line 170 spoken here.

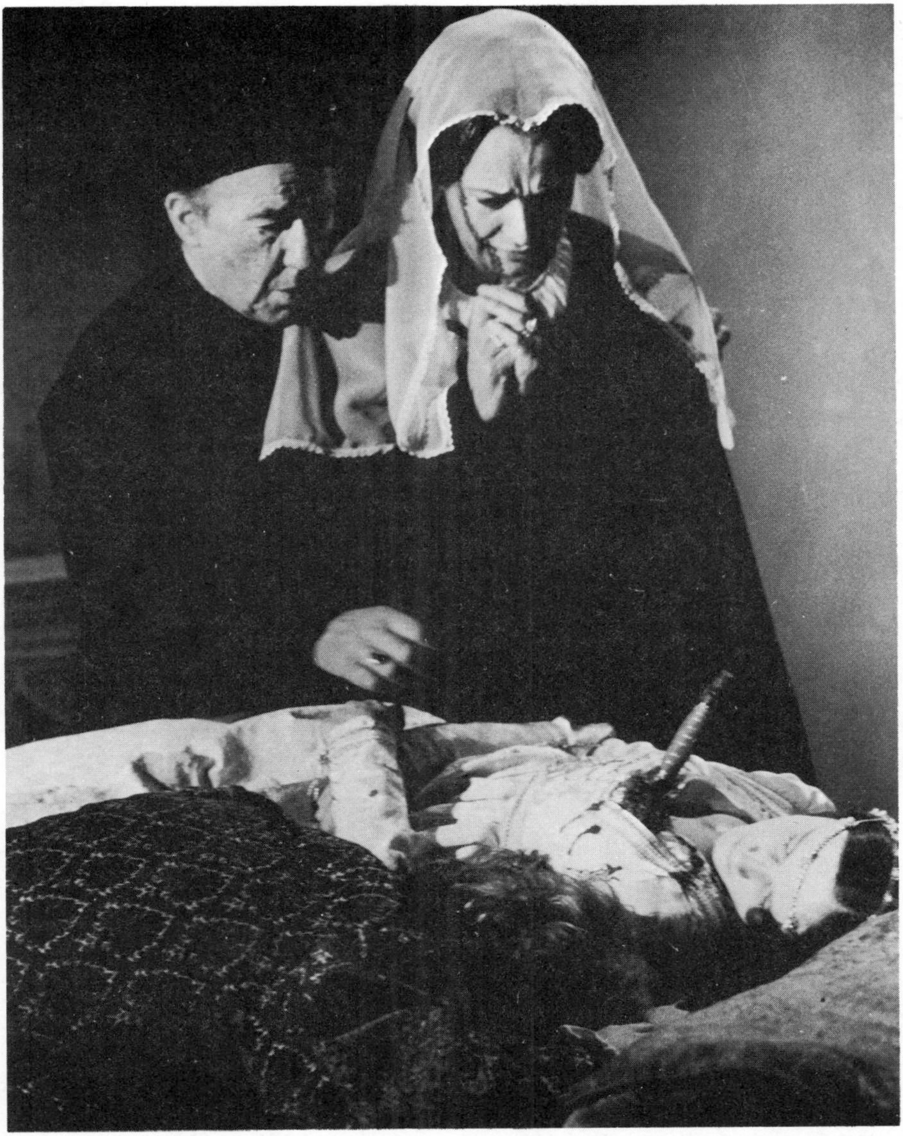

*Capulet and Lady Capulet (Michael Hordern and Jacqueline Hill) with the bodies of Romeo and Juliet (Patrick Ryecart and Rebecca Saire)*

JUL. Yea, noise? Then I'll be brief. O happy dagger!
[*Snatching Romeo's dagger.*
This is thy sheath; there rust, and let me die.
[*She stabs herself and falls on Romeo's body.*

*Enter* WATCH, *with* PARIS'S PAGE.

PAGE. This is the place; there, where the torch doth burn.

Transposed above.

I WATCH. The ground is bloody; search about the churchyard.
Go, some of you, whoe'er you find attach.
[*Exeunt some of the* WATCH.
Pitiful sight! here lies the County slain;
And Juliet bleeding, warm, and newly dead,
Who here hath lain this two days buried.
Go, tell the Prince; run to the Capulets;
Raise up the Montagues; some others search.
[*Exeunt others of the* WATCH.
We see the ground whereon these woes do lie;
But the true ground of all these piteous woes
We cannot without circumstance descry.

*Re-enter some of the* WATCH *with* BALTHASAR.

2 WATCH. Here's Romeo's man; we found him in the churchyard.
I WATCH. Hold him in safety till the Prince come hither.

Lines 173–182 omitted.

*Re-enter* FRIAR LAWRENCE *and another* WATCHMAN.

3 WATCH. Here is a friar that trembles, sighs, and weeps;
We took this mattock and this spade from him,
As he was coming from this churchyard's side.
I WATCH. A great suspicion; stay the friar too.

Lines 183–186 omitted.

*Enter the* PRINCE *and* ATTENDANTS.

PRINCE. What misadventure is so early up,
That calls our person from our morning rest?

*Enter* CAPULET, LADY CAPULET, *and* OTHERS.

SCENE 38
*Exterior. Capulet's House. Night.*

CAP. What should it be that is so shriek'd abroad?
LADY C. The people in the street cry 'Romeo',
Some 'Juliet' and some 'Paris'; and all run,
With open outcry, toward our monument.

SCENE 39
*Exterior. Verona. Churchyard. Night.*
PRINCE, FRIAR LAWRENCE, THE WATCH

PRINCE. What fear is this which startles in our ears?
I WATCH. Sovereign, here lies the County Paris slain;
And Romeo dead; and Juliet, dead before,
Warm and new kill'd.
* PRINCE. Search, seek, and know how this foul murder comes.
I WATCH. Here is a friar, and slaughter'd Romeo's man,
With instruments upon them fit to open
These dead men's tombs.

Lines 197–200 omitted.*

SCENE 40
*Interior. Verona. The The Capulets' Tomb. Night.*
CAPULET, LADY CAPULET

CAP. O heavens! O wife, look how our daughter bleeds!
This dagger hath mista'en, for, lo, his house
Is empty on the back of Montague,
And it mis-sheathed in my daughter's bosom.
LADY C. O me! this sight of death is as a bell
That warns my old age to a sepulchre.

**Insert after line 196,* 'Warm and new kill'd':
PRINCE. Seal up the mouth of outrage for a while,
Till we can clear these ambiguities.
Search, seek, and know how this foul murder comes.
Where are the parties of suspicion?

[*continued opposite*]

*Enter* MONTAGUE *and* OTHERS.

SCENE 41
*Exterior. Verona.*
*Churchyard. Night.*

PRINCE. Come, Montague, for thou art early up
To see thy son and heir more early down.
MON. Alas, my liege, my wife is dead to-night;
Grief of my son's exile hath stopp'd her breath.
What further woe conspires against mine age?
PRINCE. Look, and thou shalt see.
MON. O thou untaught! what manners is in this,
To press before thy father to a grave?

SCENE 42
*Interior. Verona.*
*The Capulets' Tomb.*
*Night.*
CAPULET, LADY CAPULET
*Enter* MONTAGUE

Lines 215–289 omitted.

PRINCE. Seal up the mouth of outrage for a while,
Till we can clear these ambiguities,
And know their spring, their head, their true descent;
And then will I be general of your woes,
And lead you even to death. Meantime forbear,
And let mischance be slave to patience.
Bring forth the parties of suspicion.
FRI. L. I am the greatest, able to do least,
Yet most suspected, as the time and place
Doth make against me, of this direful murder;
And here I stand, both to impeach and purge
Myself condemned and myself excus'd.
PRINCE. Then say at once what thou dost know in this.
FRI. L. I will be brief, for my short date of breath
Is not so long as is a tedious tale.
Romeo, there dead, was husband to that Juliet;
And she, there dead, that Romeo's faithful wife.
I married them; and their stol'n marriage-day
Was Tybalt's doomsday, whose untimely death
Banish'd the new-made bridegroom from this city
For whom, and not for Tybalt, Juliet pin'd.
You, to remove that siege of grief from her,
Betroth'd, and would have married her perforce,
To County Paris. Then comes she to me,
And with wild looks bid me devise some mean
To rid her from this second marriage,
Or in my cell there would she kill herself.
Then gave I her, so tutor'd by my art,
A sleeping potion; which so took effect
As I intended, for it wrought on her
The form of death. Meantime I writ to Romeo
That he should hither come as this dire night
To help to take her from her borrowed grave,
Being the time the potion's force should cease.
But he which bore my letter, Friar John,
Was stay'd by accident, and yesternight
Return'd my letter back. Then all alone
At the prefixed hour of her waking
Came I to take her from her kindred's vault;
Meaning to keep her closely at my cell
Till I conveniently could send to Romeo.
But when I came, some minute ere the time
Of her awakening, here untimely lay
The noble Paris and true Romeo dead.

---

FRI. L. I am the greatest, able to do least,
And here I stand, both to impeach and purge
Myself condemned and myself excus'd.
PRINCE. Then say at once what thou dost know in this.
FRI. L. Romeo, there dead, was husband to that Juliet. . . .

Lines 215–289 omitted.

She wakes ; and I entreated her come forth,
And bear this work of heaven with patience.
But then a noise did scare me from the tomb,
And she, too desperate, would not go with me,
But, as it seems, did violence on herself.
All this I know, and to the marriage
Her nurse is privy ; and if ought in this
Miscarried by my fault, let my old life
Be sacrific'd, some hour before his time,
Unto the rigour of severest law.

PRINCE. We still have known thee for a holy man.
Where's Romeo's man ? What can he say to this ?

BAL. I brought my master news of Juliet's death ;
And then in post he came from Mantua
To this same place, to this same monument.
This letter he early bid me give his father ;
And threat'ned me with death, going in the vault,
If I departed not and left him there.

PRINCE. Give me the letter, I will look on it.
Where is the County's page that rais'd the watch ?
Sirrah, what made your master in this place ?

PAGE. He came with flowers to strew his lady's grave ;
And bid me stand aloof, and so I did.
Anon comes one with light to ope the tomb ;
And by and by my master drew on him ;
And then I ran away to call the watch.

PRINCE. This letter doth make good the friar's words,
Their course of love, the tidings of her death ;
And here he writes that he did buy a poison
Of a poor pothecary, and therewithal
Came to this vault to die, and lie with Juliet.
Where be these enemies ? Capulet, Montague,
See what a scourge is laid upon your hate,
That heaven finds means to kill your joys with love !
And I, for winking at your discords too,
Have lost a brace of kinsmen. All are punish'd.

THE PRINCE *enters.*

CAP. O brother Montague, give me thy hand.
This is my daughter's jointure, for no more
Can I demand.

MON. But I can give thee more ;
For I will raise her statue in pure gold,
That whiles Verona by that name is known,
There shall no figure at such rate be set
As that of true and faithful Juliet.

CAP. As rich shall Romeo's by his lady's lie—
Poor sacrifices of our enmity !

PRINCE. A glooming peace this morning with it brings
The sun for sorrow will not show his head.
Go hence, to have more talk of these sad things ;
Some shall be pardon'd and some punished ;
For never was a story of more woe
Than this of Juliet and her Romeo. [*Exeunt.*

# GLOSSARY

Graham S. May

Difficult phrases are listed under the most important or most difficult words in them. If no such word stands out, they are listed under the first word.

Words appear in the form they take in the text. If they occur in several forms, they are listed under the root form (singular for nouns, infinitive for verbs).

Line references are given only when the same word is used with different meanings, and when there are puns.

ABROACH, (of a barrel) pierced and left flowing, i.e. 'in motion'
ABROAD, out of doors; far and wide (V iii 189)
ABUS'D, disfigured
ABUSE (n.), (i) corruption (II iii 20); (ii) crime (III i 190)
ACCIDENTS, events
ACCOUNT, (i) relation, announcement; (ii) bill, reckoning; (iii) collection (V i 45). (Pun on (i) and (ii), I v 116)
ACQUAINTANCE, 'craves acquaintance at my hand', desires to make acquaintance with me
ACTED, brought to physical consummation
ADAM CUPID, Cupid was the classical god of love. 'Adam' is prefixed perhaps as an allusion to Adam Bell, a famous outlaw archer
ADDLE, rotten
ADVENTURE, risk myself, venture (much as a Merchant Adventurer would undertake the hazards of trading overseas, II ii 84); take the risk (V iii 11)
ADVISE, 'lay hand on heart advise', take carefully to heart, and ponder, my decision
AFFECTIONS, (i) feelings (I i 124); (ii) love (II Pr 2); (iii) passion (II v 12); (iv) partiality, prejudice (III i 174); 'his own affection's counsellor', adviser of his own feelings
AFFORD, provide
AFFRAY, scare, startle
AFORE ME, As God is before me
AFTER, relying upon (I iv 8)
AGAIN, (often) 'back again'; 'for a second time' and 'in return' (II Pr 5)
AGAINST, in preparation for, by the time of (III iv 32); in preparation for the time when (IV i 113); 'against the hair', *see* HAIR
AGATE STONE, small seal-ring, often with a design of a tiny human figure cut upon it
AIRY, (i) insubstantial; (ii) 'trivial' or 'haughty' (I i 87)
ALDERMAN, high-ranking local official
ALIKE, Juliet and Romeo equally (II Pr 6)
ALL ALONG, at full length on the ground
ALLA STOCCATA CARRIES IT AWAY, (i) The Italian thrust-technique wins the day; (ii) (perhaps) Old Italian-thrust-technique (i.e. Tybalt) gets away with it
ALLOW, grant in return
ALLY, kinsman
ALONG, along with you (I i 193); 'all along', at full length
ALOOF, 'stand aloof', go and wait some way off
AMAZ'D, bewildered, dazed
AMBUSCADOES, ambushes
AMBLING, dancing
AMERCE, punish by fining
AN, if
AN IF, if
ANCIENT, i.e. which is a well-established custom (I ii 82)
ANGUISH, 'another's anguish', the smart of another pain
ANON, immediately, at once
ANSWER, (i) reply; (ii) take up a challenge; (iii) reply (to a letter); (iv) show in return. (Puns on (i), (ii), and (iii), II iv 10ff; pun on (i) and (iv), IV v 122)

ANTIC, grotesque
APE, (term of endearment) 'poor fellow'
APPERTAINING, appropriate
APPREHEND, arrest; 'apprehend thee for', arrest you on suspicion that you are
AQUA VITAE, strong spirit (such as brandy)
ARGUES, indicates
ART (n.), skill derived from learning and experience (pun on 'art' = are, II iv 87)
AS, depending how (III i 76); on (V iii 246)
ASPIR'D, mounted up to
ASSOCIATE, accompany
ATHWART, across
ATOMIES, minute particles
ATTACH, arrest
AURORA, Roman goddess of the dawn, who, as she rose each morning from the bed of her husband Tithonus, brought with her the light of day

BACK (v.), (i) give support to, (ii) turn my back on, desert. (Pun, I i 32–33)
BACKWARD TURNING, turning in the opposite direction
BAGGAGE, good-for-nothing young woman
BAK'D MEATS, pies and other pastries
BALEFUL, evil, deadly
BANDY, strike to and fro (as in tennis)
BANDYING, interchange of blows
BANQUET, light refreshment, often composed of fruit, wine and sweetmeats
BARE, destitute (V i 68)
BAREFOOT BROTHER, i.e. Franciscan friar
BARK, boat
BATING, fluttering (used of an excited hawk trying to escape its falconer's wrist)
BAUBLE, (i) short stick with a carved head carried by the professional fool; (ii) penis
BEAR (v.), (i) carry a load; (ii) copulate; (Pun on (i) and (ii), I iv 93); 'bears him', carries himself, behaves
BEAT LOVE DOWN, (i) subdue, vanquish love; (ii) lay your beloved low (i.e. have sexual intercourse with her)
BECOMED, befitting
BEETLE BROWS, overhanging eyebrows
BEFORE, ahead, in front (III iii 155); 'before and apace', run ahead, and be swift
BEFORE EASTER, i.e. during Lent (perhaps, therefore, before the new spring fashions)
BEGGARLY ACCOUNT, meagre collection
BEHESTS, commands
BEHOVEFUL, appropriate, needful
BENEDICITE, God bless you
BENEFICE, an ecclesiastical post (or 'living')
BENT OF, inclination towards
BEPAINT, colour
BESCREEN'D IN, hidden by
BESEECH, I beseech (III v 106)
BESEEMING ORNAMENTS, decorous attire
BESHREW, curse
BEST, 'at the best', i.e. the game can now only turn for the worse (*see* GAME)
BETAKE HIM TO HIS LEGS, i.e. 'disperse' or 'begin to dance'
BETHINK, consider; 'bethink you', consider this carefully
BIDE, endure
BILLS, halberds, pikes, long-handled axes
BIRD'S, maiden's
BIRTH, 'true birth', function for which it was originally created; 'birth, and heaven, and earth', i.e. his family, soul, and earthly body
BIT WITH, eaten away by (like a bud which, although it seems outwardly sound, is being invisibly consumed within by a worm)
BITE MY THUMB AT, make an insulting gesture towards (by placing the thumbnail in the mouth against the teeth, and then jerking it out, thus making a clicking sound); 'bite thee by the ear', bite you on the ear (normally a sign of affection, but Mercutio is being ironic)
BLACK, malignant (I i 139)
BLADDERS, animal bladders (used for storing liquids)
BLAZE, publicly proclaim
BLAZON, depict appropriately (used of the painting of an heraldic device)
BLIND, 'if love be blind', allusion to the theory that Cupid, the god of love, was blind
BLOWS US FROM OURSELVES, distracts us from our initial intention
BONDAGE IS HOARSE, confinement (within my father's house) and subjection (to his will) force me to whisper
BONES, 'their bones!', i.e. being slaves to the latest fad, they discard the old comfortable garments, and find that their new clothes no longer cushion the old hard seats ('benches')
BOOK, 'by th' book' (I v 108), (i) precisely, expertly; (ii) upon closely reasoned argument; (iii) making a ritual (of your kissing); strictly in accordance with a textbook of instruction (III i 99)
BOSOM, innermost thoughts and affections; 'My bosom's lord sits lightly in his throne', Love (Cupid) reigns easily in my heart

BOUND (adj.), (i) subject to legal restraint (allusion to the legal formula 'to bind over to keep the peace', meaning to threaten someone with punishment if further breach of the peace occurs), I ii 1; (ii) tied up (with pun on 'bound' = 'jump', I iv 20, and with an allusion to the Elizabethan practice of binding and imprisoning the insane in darkness as a form of treatment, I ii 54); (iii) indebted (IV ii 32); (n.), 'common bound', pun on (i) ordinary leap, (ii) ordinary limit (of height)
BOUT, dance
BOW IN THE HAMS, bend at the knees
BOW-BOY'S, Cupid's (the young archer-god of love)
BOWER, enclose
BOY, (term of abuse) mere inexperienced stripling
BRACE OF KINSMEN, a pair of my kinsmen (i.e. Mercutio and Paris)
BRAIN, 'I do bear a brain', I've a good memory yet
BREACHES, breaking into fortifications
BREAK, go bankrupt (with pun on 'cease beating'), III ii 57
BRIEF, swiftly (III iii 174)
BROAD, (i) wide; (ii) plain, evident; (iii) loose, indecent; (puns, II iv 84)
BROKE HER BROW, cut her forehead
BROKEN, cut
BURDEN, weight (i) of toil; (ii) of a husband (innuendo)
BURDEN LOVE, be a burden upon the woman you love
BURN DAYLIGHT, burn torches in daylight (proverbial expression meaning 'waste time')
BURNS OUT, extinguishes (by using up the available fuel)
BUSINESS, affairs which call them from home (II ii 16)
BUT, (often) 'only'; without (I Pr 11); unless, except (I i 233); 'unless' or 'provided that' (II ii 76); 'but saying over', I only say again; 'knows not but', is entirely under the impression that
BUTT-SHAFT, blunt-headed arrow (used in shooting at a practice-target or 'butt')
BY, near (I ii 94); 'cast by', cast aside
BY TH' ROOD, by the Cross (on which Christ died)
BY'R LADY, By Our Lady (the Virgin Mary)

CAITIFF WRETCH, poor miserable wretch (who)
CAKES OF ROSES, compressed bundles of rose-leaves (used as perfume)
CALL . . . IN QUESTION, summon to mind
CALLS DEATH, deems worthy of death
CALLS OUT ON, summons
CANCELL'D, rendered invalid (by the death of Tybalt and the banishment of Romeo)
CANDLE-HOLDER, attendant who holds the light (hence 'mere onlooker
CANDLES, 'Night's candles', the stars
CANKER, worm that eats into and destroys plants
CANK'RED, 'corrupted by ulcers', hence 'cank'red with peace', rusted through disuse; 'cank'red hate', spiteful enmity
CANOPY, covering suspended over a bed
CAPEL'S, of the Capulets
CARE TO STAY, concern, anxiety, about what will happen if I stay
CAREFUL, provident on your behalf
CARRIAGE, (i) moral or bodily deportment; (ii) sexual skill (pun)
CARRY COALS, i.e. 'perform menial work', hence 'be humiliated'
CASE, (i) state of affairs; (ii) mask (I iv 29); (iii) predicament (II iv 50, III iii 84); (iv) container for a musical instrument (with pun on (i), IV v 98)
CATLING, a piece of cat-gut used to make a lute-string
CAUSE, 'a gentleman . . . of the first and second cause', a man expert in and punctilious about the theoretical management of quarrelling ('cause' here being a term for the gradations by which a formal quarrel was conceived to develop)
CENTRE, i.e. Juliet. Romeo sees his body as the heavy or 'dull' element, which, as it is subject to the force of gravitation, is irresistibly pulled towards the centre of the earth (Romeo's heart), and hence towards Juliet (for Juliet is in his heart)
CHALLENGE, assert his claim upon
CHANGE, passing (of the seasons) (I ii 9)
CHANGE EYES, exchange eyes (allusion to the popular theory that the contrast between the beauty of the toad's eyes and the insignificance of those of the lark indicated that they had exchanged them)
CHARGE (n.), important, weighty matters
CHARNEL HOUSE, outbuilding attached to a church, in which skulls and bones which had been removed from old graves were stored
CHEER (n.), (festive) food, provisions

CHEERLY, cheerily, heartily
CHEVERIL, kid leather, i.e. easily stretched
CHIDE AWAY, drive away
CHINKS, the sound made by coins striking each other, i.e. 'money'
CHOLER, anger; 'in choler'; angry (with pun on COLLAR)
CHOPT LOGIC!, fallacious reasoning (is being) bandied backwards and forwards!
CHURL, niggard, miser
CIRCLE, (i) magical circle within which a magician confines dangerous spirits; (ii) vagina (innuendo)
CIRCUMSTANCE, detailed information; 'stay the circumstance', await the details
CITY SIDE, city's edge
CIVIL, (i) belonging to citizens; (ii) occurring among citizens of the same town (I Pr 4, I i 87); (iii) seemly, decorous (III ii 10)
CLASPS, (i) fastenings of book covers; (ii) embraces (of a wife) (pun)
CLOSE (adj.), reticent, secretive (I i 147); private, cramped (II ii 189); 'close curtain', 'shut' or 'concealing' curtain of darkness; (adv.), hand to hand (I i 105); (v.), join (II vi 6)
CLOSELY, secretly
CLOSET, private chamber
CLOUT, rag, fragment of cloth
COCK-A-HOOP, 'set cock-a-hoop', cast off all restraint, start unlimited uproar
COCKATRICE, mythical animal that could kill with one glance of its eyes
COIL, fuss
COLLAR, hangman's noose
COLLIERS, i.e. 'mere dirty coal-tradesmen' (puns on 'colliers', 'choler', 'collar', I i 2ff)
COMBINE, 'all combin'd', all united in harmony
COME ABOUT, eventually come true
COME NEAR, struck home, hit upon the truth
COMEST TO AGE, come of age, reach maturity
COMFORT, happiness (III iii 165)
COMFORTABLE, comfort-bringing
COMMISSION, delegated authority for the performance of a judicial function
COMPARE, 'past compare', beyond comparison; 'with above compare', as being beyond comparison
COMPASS, range
COMPLIMENT, formal civility, etiquette
CONCEALED LADY, secret wife
CONCEIT, thought; 'Conceit more rich in matter . . . ornament', Imagination, when what it conceives is more real and powerful than words can express, rejoices in this body of real feeling, and does not bother to find a necessarily inadequate expression for what it feels in words, which would be merely ornamental and unable to express the fundamental core of feeling
CONCEIVE, understand
CONDUCT, guide; guidance (III iii 131)
CONDUIT, fountain (here, in the shape of a human figure)
CONFIDENCE, 'confidential conversation', or perhaps a malapropism for 'conference'
CONFOUNDS, destroys
CONFUSION'S, disaster's; 'these confusions', this disorderly behaviour
CONJURATION, solemn entreaty
CONJURE, summon a spirit by uttering magical spells (Mercutio parodies this process, II i 6–21); 'conjure down', dismiss spirits (with innuendo)
CONSORT, (i) associate; (ii) play or sing in harmony (pun on (i) and (ii), III i 43); (iii) attend, accompany (III i 127)
CONTENT, I iii 85, (i) contents (of a book); (ii) satisfaction, contentment
CONTRACT, exchange of vows
CONTRARY (v.), contradict
CONVOY, conveyance
COP'ST, 'that cop'st with', (you) who are prepared to encounter
CORDIAL, restorative, comforting medicine
CORSE, corpse
COST, 'for cost', for fear of (excessive) expense
COT-QUEEN, a man who meddles with a housewife's domestic affairs
COUNSEL, (i) advice; (ii) private speech (I iii 9); (iii) self-communing (II ii 53); 'good counsel', an effective plan resulting from deliberation or advice (I i 141); 'keep counsel', maintain secrecy
COUNTERVAIL, balance, outweigh
COUNTY, count
COURSE, (i) voyage (i.e. life) (I iv 112); (ii) procedure, action; 'their course of love', the progress of their love
COURT-CUBBERT, movable sideboard used to display plate
COURTSHIP, (i) courtly existence; (ii) wooing
COVER (n.), (i) binding of a book; (ii) wife; (pun on (i) and (ii), I iii 89); (iii) vehicle-hood (I iv 60)
COVERT, concealment, shelter

COZ, cousin (used indiscriminately for any close kin)
CREATE, 'of nothing first create', initially created out of nothing at all
CRIES, 'on Romeo cries', cries out against Romeo
CROSS (adj.), perverse; (v.), interfere with
CROTCHETS, 'carry no crotchets', endure none of your caprices (pun on 'crotchets' = quarter notes in music)
CROW, crowbar (V ii 21)
CROW-KEEPER, (i) boy employed to keep fields free from crows; (ii) scarecrow
CRUSH, drink off
CULL'D, chosen, picked out
CULLING OF SIMPLES, picking out ingredients (for herbal medicines)
CUNNING, skilful
CUPID, the classical blind boy-god of love (often a person playing the role of Cupid would act as the presenter or 'excuser' of such maskers as those of I iv)
CUPID'S ARROW, (i) an arrow from the bow of Cupid, whose arrows had the power to make whomsoever they struck fall violently in love; (ii) a penis (innuendo)
CURES WITH, is cured by
CURFEW BELL, (here) bell rung at 3 or 4 a.m.
CURIOUS, inquisitive
CUTS BEAUTY OFF, i.e. denies her the opportunity of passing on her beauty to her offspring, and thereby preserving it
CYNTHIA'S, the moon-goddess Diana's

DARE, (i) show courage; (ii) challenge; 'how he dares being dared', how courageous he can show himself to be when challenged
DATE, 'fearful date', period of existence full of fear; 'date of breath', allotted period of life; 'the date is out with such prolixity', the custom of wasting so many words is now out of date
DATELESS BARGAIN, agreement that is everlasting (with no date of termination)
DEAL DOUBLE, deceive
DEAR, (i) beloved; (ii) expensive (puns at I v 45 and I v 116)
DEATH-MARK'D, (i) preordained for death; (ii) disfigured with deaths
DEFENCE, means of defending yourself (i.e. the gunpowder)
DEMESNES, (i) domains, regions; (ii) estates, lands ((i) and (ii), II i 20; (ii) only, III v 181)
DEN, 'good den', good evening or afternoon
DEPEND, impend, cast an ominous and ill-omened shadow
DESCENT, sequence
DESPERATE, (i) despairing; (ii) violent, reckless (III iii 108)
DESPITE, 'in despite', in defiance or contempt
DETERMINE OF, (i) decide between; (ii) put an end to
DEVISE, imagine, guess (III i 68)
DEW-DROPPING, water-precipitating, rainy (i.e. more responsive than the 'frozen' north)
DIAN'S WIT, the intelligence (to remain chaste and free from the passion of love) of Diana, goddess of chastity
DIDO, Queen of Carthage, a famous beauty who (according to Virgil's *Aeneid*), when deserted by her lover Aeneas, burnt herself to death upon a funeral pyre
DIFFERENT GREETING, (violent) clash of opposites
DIGRESSING, if it departs
DISCOVER, reveal
DISCOVERY, (i) investigation; (ii) revealing (his feelings)
DISCREET, self-controlled (i.e. sane)
DISHCLOUT, dishcloth (in comparison)
DISLIKE, 'thee dislike', is unpleasant to you
DISPARAGEMENT, indignity
DISPATCH, swiftly put an end to, kill
DISPLANT, uproot
DISPUTE WITH THEE OF, discuss (philosophically) with you
DISTEMPERED, unbalanced, disordered
DISTEMP'RATURE, mental disturbance
DISTILLED, extracted
DIVERS KIND, various kinds
DIVISION, (i) trill, or rapid succession of musical notes; (ii) separation (between the lovers) (pun)
DO SOME GOOD ON, have a good effect on
DOFF, take off, lay aside
DOOM (n.), judgement; 'general doom', Day of Judgement; (v.), condemn (you) to
DOOMSDAY, (i) the Day of Judgement (III iii 10); (ii) day of death (V iii 233)
DOST, 'what dost thou with', what have you to do with
DOTH, do (I Pr 8)
DOUBT, suspect (V iii 44)
DOVES DRAW LOVE, allusion to the chariot of Venus, classical goddess of love, which was supposed to be drawn through the air by doves given to her by Juno, wife of Jupiter

DOWN, (i) in bed; (ii) laid low in death (pun, V iii 208); 'down so late', so late going to bed; 'down again', gone back to sleep again

DOWNRIGHT, 'It rains downright', it rains (i.e. Juliet weeps) indeed, in fullest measure

DRAM, (i) small measure (actually $\frac{1}{8}$ fluid ounce) of medicine; (ii) small draught or dose of spirits (here, poison)

DRAW, (i) 'unsheathe swords for action', and hence 'threaten'; (ii) withdraw (pun on (i) and (ii), I i 3–4); 'draws him on', draws his sword and threatens

DRAWER, tapster, one who 'draws' the ale in an inn

DRAWN, with drawn sword; 'drawn with', pulled by

DRIFT, meaning (II iii 55); intention, plan (IV i 114)

DRIVELLING, (i) slavering; (ii) talking nonsense

DROWN'D, suffused with tears

DRY SORROW DRINKS OUR BLOOD, allusion to the theory that sorrow caused the heart to drain all the blood from the veins into itself

DRY-BEAT, cudgel without drawing blood

DUCAT, small gold or silver coin

DUG, breast

DUMP, sorrowful tune

DUMPS, low spirits

DUN, I iv 41, quasi-proper name for 'horse'. Allusion to (i) the phrase 'Dun is in the mire', meaning 'things are at a standstill; and (ii) a Christmas game in which one tried to pull a log (representing a horse) from an imaginary mire

DUN'S THE MOUSE, THE CONSTABLE'S OWN WORD, (literally) 'the mouse is dark brown' (i.e. well-camouflaged), as is the distinctive saying of the officer of the peace' (i.e. 'Be as inconspicuous as a mouse', with a pun upon 'done', I iv 31)

DWELL ON FORM, make a point of formal etiquette

EARTH, (i) i.e. death (I ii 14); (ii) earthly body (III ii 59, III iii 120); 'She is the hopeful lady of my earth', perhaps (i) Juliet is the promising only daughter of my body; or (ii) Juliet is the hopeful sole potential mistress of my inheritance; or (iii) Juliet is the mistress of my world, is all the world to me; 'dull earth', Romeo's body, which is (i) melancholy, (ii) heavy (*see* CENTRE); 'to the earth', to the earth's inhabitants (II iii 18); 'on earth', alive (*see* MY HUSBAND) (III v 206)

EARTH-TREADING STARS, beautiful women who, as they walk, will illuminate the night like stars

ECHO, 'cave where Echo lies', allusion to Ovid's tale (*Metamorphoses* iii) of the nymph Echo who, frustrated in her amorous pursuit of Narcissus, hid in a cave for shame, and pined away until only her echoing voice was left

EFFECT, result (i.e. fulfilment) (I v 104)

EITHER, 'either part', the two factions; 'in either', from the other

ELF-LOCKS, tangles caused by the fairies

ELL, a measure of forty-five inches

ELSE, in addition (I i 191)

ENDART, pierce with (as with an arrow)

ENGROSSING DEATH, (i) death who buys up all, monopolises; (ii) (perhaps) death who writes out ('engrosses') the legal document (with which the bargain is ratified) (possible pun)

ENPIERCED, transfixed, pierced through

ENSIGN, badge, heraldic emblem, banner

ENTREAT THE TIME ALONE, ask you to leave us alone for this while

ENVIRONED WITH, surrounded by

ESTATE, predicament, condition

ET CETERA, pudenda

ETHIOP'S, (black) African's

EXCUSE (n.), explanation for our uninvited presence at the ball (I iv 1). The entrance of unexpected disguised guests at a masked ball was customarily preceded by a formal speech of introduction

EXECUTION, manner of proceeding

EXHALES, draws forth (Meteors were thought to be vapours drawn from the earth, and then ignited, by the sun)

EXPIRE THE TERM, bring to an end the limited period (legal metaphor: Romeo sees himself as having entered into a legal contract from this evening for a mortgage, but feels it to be inevitable that he will exceed the limit of time within which it should be repaid, and that he will thus incur a forfeit, in this case, death)

EXTREMES, utmost difficulties, horrible afflictions

FACE, 'to my face', (i) to myself directly; (ii) about my face (pun)

FAIN, gladly, willingly

FAIR, fair woman (I i 234, II Pr 3); 'fair according', favourably agreeing, consenting
FAITH, 'in faith', in truth; 'my faith in heaven', my marriage vow is registered in heaven (*see* MY HUSBAND)
FALL BACKWARD, (i) tumble backward; (ii) make love (innuendo)
FALL'N OUT, happened
FANTASTICOES, absurd, ridiculous fops
FASHION-MONGERS, those who avidly follow the latest fashions
FAST, sound asleep (IV v 1)
FATAL, deadly, producing death; fraught with evil destiny (I Pr 5)
FAULT, lack, want (II iv 119)
FAY, faith; 'by my fay', indeed
FEAR, 'fear me not', don't doubt me; 'I fear thee!', as if I would be afraid of you! (pun)
FEARFUL, (i) causing fear (II Pr 8); (ii) apprehensive, anxious (III iii 1, III v 3)
FEASTING PRESENCE, large reception-room in a great house arranged for a feast
FEE SIMPLE, absolute legal possession (in this case, of only an hour and a quarter's duration)
FEEL, 'feel no love in this', am not requited with love in return; 'feel the loss but not the friend Which you weep for', feel strongly the presence in your own mind of a sense of loss, but not experience the actual presence (alive) of him for whom you weep
FEELING, deeply felt (III v 74)
FEIGN AS, act as if
FEST'RING, rotting, corrupting
FETTLE, prepare, make ready
FIDDLESTICK, bow with which a fiddle is played (here, 'sword')
FIE, for shame (exclamation of disgust or contempt)
FIELD-BED, (i) camp-bed; (ii) bed on the ground (pun)
FIGURE, form, sculptured image
FILM, gossamer
FIND, I ii 41–2, (i) look for; (ii) interpret, read (pun)
FINE, penalty
FIR'D, ignited
FISHIFIED, (i) compared to a herring; (ii) made a mere 'fish', i.e. inferior meat, cold and bloodless
FLASK, horn for carrying gunpowder
FLATTERING-SWEET, so pleasant as to arouse a suspicion that the pleasure is deceptive
FLATTERING TRUTH OF SLEEP, pleasing but perhaps deceptive revelations of dreams
FLECKEL'D, dappled
FLEER, sneer, mock
FLESH, meat, i.e. human flesh (II iv 37); 'get thyself in flesh', grow fat; 'pretty piece of flesh', (i) fine creature; (ii) fine piece of meat (pun)
FLIES, parasites
FLINT, i.e. of the pavement
FLIRT-GILLS, loose girls
FLOWER'D, perforated in an ornamental fashion, i.e. 'pinked' (*see* PINK). Hence, as 'pink' is the name of a flower, it is 'flower'd' (puns)
FLOW'D IN, (i) lamented in, wept in; (ii) was eloquent in (*see* PETRARCH)
FLOW'RING FACE, allusion to the frequent practice of depicting the serpent in Eden with a human face surrounded by flowers
FOLLOW ME, cap for me (II iv 60)
FOLLOWER, 'he'll be your follower', (i) he will readily follow to fight with you; (ii) he will be your attendant, servant
FOND, (i) excessively affectionate; (ii) foolish
FOOL, term of endearment (I iii 32); 'Fortune's fool', (i) Fortune's dupe; (ii) a professional fool or jester kept and employed by Fortune to entertain her
FOOL'S PARADISE, happiness based upon an illusion
FOOT IT, step lively
FOR, inclined towards (III iv 38); to be (III ii 134); 'for you', ready to fight you; 'For all this same', in spite of all this
FORFEIT, penalty (i.e. execution) (I i 97); 'pay the forfeit of the peace', (i) pay the penalty (for the violation) of the peace; or (ii) pay for the violation ('forfeit') of the peace
FORM, II iv 33, (i) etiquette; (ii) bench (pun); V iii 245, appearance; 'form of wax', wax model (lacking true humanity)
FORSOOTH, in truth
FORSWORN, abjured, sworn to refuse (I i 221); perjured (III v 237); 'I'll not be forsworn', I will not break my word (i.e. (i) to you that I will renounce you; or (ii) to Paris, that you will marry him)
FORTH, forth from (I i 117); 'They are all forth', all the servants are out of the house (and thus cannot answer Capulet's call of IV ii 43)
FRANK, generous, lavish
FRAY, disturbance, brawl
FRIEND, (i) lover (III v 43); (ii) kinsman (III

iii 151, III v 75); (Juliet's secret pun on (i) and (ii), III v 77)

FRIGHT YOU UP, frighten, startle you into getting up (with possible innuendo)

FROM FORTH, from (I Pr 5); out of the way of (II iii 4)

FUME, (i) smoke; (ii) unsubstantial substance which rises to the head and clouds the mental faculties

FURY, (i) anger; (ii) (perhaps) an avenging tormenting spirit from Hell

'GAINST, in preparation for; by the time of

GALL, (i) bitter poison (I i 192); (ii) bitterness (I v 90)

GAME, I iv 39, (i) bout of gambling; (ii) quarry (pun); 'The game was ne'er so fair and I am done', allusion to the gambling proverb 'When play is best, it's time to leave', i.e., leave while the going is good

GAPES, longs (open-mouthed)

GEAR, goings-on (II iv 96); substance, stuff (V i 60)

GENERAL (n.), leader

GHOSTLY, spiritual

GI'GO'DEN, grant you good afternoon (or good evening)

GIPSY, allusion to the theory that gipsies were thought to be Egyptian in origin (Cleopatra was Queen of Egypt)

GIVE IT YOU, pay you back, retaliate

GIVE LEAVE, leave us alone

GIVE YOU, call you

GLEEK, mock (to 'give someone the gleek' was to make a jest at someone's expense)

GO TO, come now

GOD-DEN, good afternoon or good evening

GOD-I-GODEN, God give you good evening (impatient exclamation)

GOD SHIELD I SHOULD DISTURB, God defend me from disturbing

GOD YE, God give you

GOD'S BREAD, consecrated bread used in the Communion Service

GOES TO THE WALL, gives way in conflict, submits, fails (proverbial)

GONE, dead people (V iii 60)

GOOD THOU, good fellow

GOODMAN BOY, yeoman (i.e. no gentleman) youngster (i.e. mere immature boy)

GOOSE, (*see* WITH), II iv 72, (i) prostitute; (ii) simpleton; 'sweet goose', (i) tasty cooked goose; (ii) dear but silly friend (*see* WILD-GOOSE CHASE)

GORE-BLOOD, clotted blood

GOSSIP, (i) friend; (ii) chattering woman who delights in idle talk

GRACE, (i) favour (I iii 60); (ii) beneficent virtue (II iii 15); (iii) capacity to receive divine grace (II iii 28)

GRANT, 'though grant', though they may respond by granting (the prayer)

GRAVE, III i 95, (i) solemn; (ii) buried (pun)

GRAVITY, profound, serious speech (ironic)

GRAZE, feed

GREATEST, i.e. most liable to suspicion

GREEN, 'sick and green', sickly and wan-looking, with possible allusion to 'green sickness' (*see below*)

GREEN-SICKNESS CARRION, pallid, immature, and worthless creature ('carrion' literally denotes putrefying decayed flesh, and 'green-sickness' denotes an anaemic disease which particularly afflicts young girls at puberty)

GRIEVE, (i) vex, anger; (ii) weigh down (by the sad fact of his absence)

GRIPING, 'when griping grief', when agonising sorrow (quotation from a poem in praise of music printed in *The Paradise of Dainty Devices*, 1576)

GROUND, (i) earth; (ii) reason; (pun, V iii 178–9)

GROW, i.e. become pregnant

GRUB, insect larva (which burrows into nuts)

GYVES, fetters, shackles

HAIR, 'against the hair', against (i) my inclination; (ii) the pubic hair

HALL, 'a hall', let's have some room for dancing

HAND, 'with one hand beats old death aside . . . back to', either (i) metaphorical; or (ii) 'parried Tybalt's thrust with the dagger in his left hand, and riposted (thrust back in turn) with the rapier in his right'; 'at my hand', with me; 'at your hands', when communicated directly by you

HANG UP, thrust aside as useless (like out-of-use armour hung upon a wall)

HANGING IN THE STARS, (already) astrologically fore-ordained by the configuration of the stars, but not yet brought into action upon the earth

HAP, 'dear hap', good fortune

HAPLY, with luck; perhaps

HAPPY, opportune (V iii 168); 'in happy time', how opportune and lucky!

HARE, (i) the animal; (ii) prostitute (pun on the sound of 'whore')

HARLOTRY, good-for-nothing hussy

HATE, 'damned hate', malicious suicide (seen as incurring damnation, as suicide was considered to be a mortal sin)

HAVE AT, 'Have at thee' and 'have at you', take this! (i.e. I shall attack)

HAVING, 'that which having', that which, once in one's possession

HAVIOUR, behaviour

HAY, thrust home, thrust through

HEAD, 'I have a head, sir, that will find out logs', (i) I am particularly good at finding logs; (ii) I am a logger-head (blockhead)

HEALTHS, toasts of wine

HEART, fellow (I i 182, I v 84); 'My heart is full of woe', perhaps an allusion to a line from the ballad, 'A Pleasant New Ballad of Two Lovers'

HEARTLESS HINDS, (i) cowardly yokels; (ii) (with pun on 'hart' = stag and 'hind' = female deer) mere female deer who have no stag to protect them

HEART'S EASE, title of a contemporary popular tune

HEAVY, (i) heavy in weight, sturdy; (ii) heavy in spirit, mournful; (pun, I i 135, I iv 12)

HEEL, 'on the heel', close behind

HELD HIM CARELESSLY, valued him, loved him, but little

HELEN, Helen of Troy (wife of Menelaus of Sparta, and whose abduction by Paris was the cause of the Trojan War), renowned for her supreme beauty

HERO, of Sestos, loved by Leander, who nightly swam the Hellespont to visit her until he finally drowned

HIGH-ALONE, upright on her own

HIGHMOST, highest (i.e. it is noon)

HILDING, worthless good-for-nothing

HINDS, (i) yokels; (ii) female deer; (pun)

HIST, (i) exclamation to enjoin Romeo's silence, attract his attention, and call upon him to listen; (ii) (perhaps) a falconer's call to attract his falcon

HIT (n.), (i) shot (of an arrow), attempt; (ii) verbal attempt, guess; (v.), (i) struck with an arrow (innuendo, I i 205ff); (ii) guess (II iii 41)

HOAR, (i) mouldy; (ii) grey- or white-haired with age; (iii) (pun on the sound of 'whore') 'whore' or 'whorish'

HOARS, (i) grows stale, old, mouldy; (ii) 'whores' (pun)

HOLIDAM, i.e. 'halidom', (i) holiness; (ii) holy place or relic; (iii) Our Lady (the Virgin Mary)

HOLP, helped

HOMELY, straightforward

HONEST, honourable; respectable, chaste (II i 28)

HOOD, (of a hawk) 'blindfold', hence 'pacify', 'tame'

HOOD-WINK'D, blind-folded

HOOKS, fish-hooks

HOPEFUL, inspiring hope

HOT, (i) eager (II v 62); (ii) violently raging (III i 137); (iii) irascible, violently-tempered (III v 175)

HOUR, 'in the hour', at hourly intervals

HOUSE (n.), often 'household', 'family'; sheath (the dagger was often worn in a sheath behind one's back), V iii 202; 'of the very first house', from the very best school of instruction; 'here comes of the house', here come some of the household; (v.), dwell

HUMOROUS, (i) damp; (ii) whimsical, capricious, full of 'humours' (moods)

HUMOUR, (i) mood, inclination; (ii) whim, caprice; (iii) fluid (here, that would make one drowsy), IV i 96; 'humours!', i.e. 'Mr Moody, Mr Caprice!'

HUNTING THEE HENCE WITH HUNTS-UP, rousing you up to go with some such tune as 'Hunt's Up'. (Allusion to the custom of awakening couples on the morning after their marriage by blowing horns. 'Hunt's Up', originally 'The Hunt Is Up', was a hunting-song for the early morning)

HURDLE, frame or sledge upon which traitors would be publicly drawn through the streets on their way to execution

HUSWIFE, housewife

I, III ii 45ff, series of puns on (i) I (the personal pronoun); (ii) ay (= yes); (iii) eye ('those eyes' = Romeo's eyes)

I AM FOR YOU, I shall answer you (accept your challenge) without hesitation

ILL, 'none ill', no bad ones

ILL-BESEEMING, (i) unbefitting (I v 72); (ii) unnatural (III iii 113)

ILL-DIVINING, apprehensive, having a presentiment of evil

IMPEACH AND PURGE . . . EXCUS'D, to accuse myself (already condemned by myself) and to clear myself from guilt (being already accused of guilt by myself)

IMPORT (n.), 'dear import', serious importance; (v.), signify, seem to presage
INDITE, i.e. 'invite' (deliberate malapropism to mock the Nurse's own)
INHERIT, receive
INSTRUMENTS, musical instruments (IV v 86)
INTERCESSION, petition on someone else's behalf
IRON WIT, dull or stupid wit
ISSUE OF TRUE HONOUR, truly honourable solution
ISSUING, pouring
ITCH, 'my fingers itch', i.e. for the opportunity of striking you

JACK, (i) insolent, low fellow (II iv 142, IV v 141); (ii) fellow (III i 11)
JAUNCE, tiring journey
JAUNCING, prancing
JEALOUS, suspicious
JEALOUS-HOOD, jealous woman (or perhaps 'Miss Jealousy')
JOINER-SQUIRREL, squirrel with teeth like a chisel ('joiner' = carpenter)
JOIN-STOOLS, stools made by a joiner (i.e. 'well-made stools')
JOINTURE, 'This is my daughter's jointure', this (my grasping your hand in friendship) is the only marriage-settlement that my daughter shall receive from you
JOVE LAUGHS, Jupiter laughs (proverbial, ultimately deriving from Ovid's *Ars Amatoria* (*The Art of Love*), i 633: 'Jupiter from on high laughs at the perjuries of lovers')
JOYS, i.e. offspring (Romeo and Juliet) (V iii 292)

KEEP, III ii 74, (i) dwell in; (ii) guard (as dragons were supposed to stand watch over treasure); perform regularly (V iii 16)
KEEPERS, nurses (or gaolers)
KINDLY, aptly, exactly
KING COPHETUA, probable allusion to a popular ballad about this supposedly African king which (as the title of one version which survives in the *Collection of Old Ballads* of 1723 puts it) tells of '*Cupid's Revenge*, or an account of a king who slighted all women, and at length was constrained to marry a beggar, who proved a fair and virtuous queen'
KING OF CATS, *see* PRINCE OF CATS
KINSMAN, (i) relative by birth; (ii) relative by marriage (i.e. 'husband') (III v 95)
KNAVES, (i) servants; (ii) rogues
KNOT, i.e. of marriage
KNOW, 'I know what', I know what I am doing

LABEL, 'Shall be the label to another deed', shall be joined in marriage to that of Paris, just as a waxen seal (already applied in ratification of the legal document ('deed') of her marriage to Romeo) should be affixed upon another such 'deed' (of marriage to Paris) to ratify it
LADY, 'God's lady dear', the dear Virgin Mary; 'lady, lady, lady', ironic allusion to the refrain of an old ballad about an exemplarily fair and virtuous lady
LADYBIRD, (i) term of endearment; (ii) 'a woman inconstant in love' or 'harlot' (the sudden realisation of this ambiguity is the cause of the Nurse's embarrassed retraction of the term in the 'God forbid!' of I iii 4)
LAID, II i 26, (i) caused (the spirit) to disappear; (ii) caused the erection to subside (innuendo); 'laid wormwood to', placed wormwood, (the juice of) a plant of proverbially bitter taste, upon
LAMMAS-EVE, the evening of 31 July
LAMMAS-TIDE, 1 August, a harvest festival of the early English Church
LANGUISH, sickness, suffering
LANTERN, (i) lighthouse; (ii) architectural structure in a roof in the form of a tower with apertures letting in light; (iii) lamp
LAST, mould around which a shoemaker constructs a shoe
LASTING LABOUR, endless toil
LATE, recently (III iv 24); 'of late', recently
LAURA . . . BERHYME HER, Laura de Noves (Petrarch's chaste beloved whom he celebrated in his sonnets), compared with Romeo's beloved, was a mere kitchen-girl – although it is true that she had a lover who was a better poet (or 'better lover') to celebrate her in verse
LAY, bet (I iii 13); 'lay hand on heart advise', take carefully to heart, and ponder, my decision; 'lay knife aboard', (i) stake a claim upon her (as a diner at an 'ordinary' (restaurant) would bring his own cutlery and place it upon the table to reserve a place for himself); (ii) attack (with a knife)
LEARN, teach; 'learnt me', taught myself
LEAVE, 'give me leave', let me alone; 'leave it for', leave instruction that it should be

LENTEN PIE, (i) a pie for Lent, hence without meat; (ii) (perhaps) a meat pie mouldy through prolonged surreptitious nibbling throughout Lent

LEVEL, line of aim

LICK, ''tis an idle cook that cannot lick his fingers', proverbial: a bad cook would not wish to taste the food he has himself prepared

LIEF, 'had as lief', would as willingly

LIGHT (adj.), (i) immodest (II ii 99, II ii 105, with pun on 'dark'); (ii) trivial (II vi 20); (n.), 'bear the light', (i) carry something light in weight; (ii) carry the torch (and hence avoid having to dance); (pun)

LIGHTNESS, (i) light weight; (ii) triviality, frivolity (pun)

LIGHTS (v.), alights, descends

LIMITS, boundaries, (here) boundary-walls

LINEAMENT, line or feature

LISPING, with affected speech

LIST, 'as they list', however they like

LIVER, 'the longer liver take all', proverbial cheery phrase originally meaning (i) the survivor (of a group of joint-tenants) will get the whole property; (ii) Death (the 'longer liver' as himself undying) will get everyone in the end. Here it means something like 'Live merrily, for nothing matters after death

LIVERY, uniform, distinctive dress

LIVING (n.), property, means of living

LODGING, night's resting-place

LOGGER-HEAD, blockhead, idiot

LOLLING, with tongue (or 'bauble') hanging out

LONG SWORD, old-fashioned, out of date, two-handed sword

LOOK, 'look about', take care, get busy; 'look to', take care of; 'look to like', (i) visually examine with a view to liking; (ii) expect to like; 'look'd not for', did not anticipate or seek

LOUR, look angry

LOVE-PERFORMING, that brings about (or 'in order to bring about') the consummation of love

LOVE'S WEAK CHILDISH BOW, the bow of Cupid, the boy-god of love, whose bow had the power to drive whoever was struck by one of its arrows to fall violently in love

LOVING-JEALOUS OF HIS LIBERTY, so loving the bird that it wishes to give it pleasure by allowing it liberty, but fears to lose it by granting it too much

LUSTY, vigorous, lively

MADE, went (I ii 222); 'what made your master', what was your master doing?

MAID, 'her maid', a maiden who is a follower of the moon, and who hence is chaste, as Diana (the moon-goddess) was the goddess of chastity

MAKE AGAINST, give evidence against

MAKES DAINTY, acts fastidious, coy, is loth (to dance)

MAMMET, doll, puppet

MAN, man of honour, a valiant man (III i 57); 'You'll be the man!', you want to play the role of the big fellow!; 'Here comes my man', here comes the man I was looking for (with pun on 'man' = manservant)

MANAGE (n.), course, conduct; (v.), manipulate, wield

MANDRAKES', those of the mandrake plant (whose forked roots made it resemble the human figure, and which was said to utter a human cry of pain if uprooted, a cry which would kill or drive insane whoever pulled it from the ground)

MAR, 'himself to mar', (i) for God Himself to spoil; (ii) but he (Romeo) spoiled or marred himself; (iii) in order that he (Romeo) might spoil himself

MARCHPANE, marzipan

MARGENT, summary or explanatory notes often written in the margin of a text

MARK (n.), target (innuendo); 'God save the mark', phrase used as a recognition of and apology for something disagreeable; (v.), listen, attend to; 'mark thee to', designate you for

MARKMAN, marksman

MARRIED LINEAMENT, harmoniously blended line or feature

MARRY, indeed; 'Marry, come up', exclamation of indignant or amused surprise or contempt

MASK, masked ball

MASK'D, attended a masked ball

MASKERS, disguised revellers at a masked ball

MASKS, black visors, half-masks occasionally worn in public by women of quality

MASS, 'evening mass', possibly 'mass', but more probably merely 'divine service'

MATCH, 'cry a match', claim a victory

MATCH'D, compared (II Pr 4); provided with a husband (III v 179)

MATTOCK, tool, a combination of spade and pick for loosening hard ground

MAW, stomach

MEAN (n.), means, method (with pun on 'mean' = poor, base, III iii 45)
MEANS, abilities, opportunities are (II Pr 11); way, i.e. poison (III v 103); 'by any means', (i) in any way; (ii) through any intermediaries
MEANT LOVE, intended to be love
MEASURE (n.), I v 48, (i) portion, measured amount; (ii) stately formal dance; (pun); measurement (III iii 70); (v.), (i) weigh, judge; (ii) mete out for, apportion to; (pun)
MEAT, (i) food (III i 21, III i 104); (ii) whore (pun on (i) and (ii), II iv 132)
MEDICINE, medicine has
MEDLAR, (i) a tree whose fruit resembles the female sexual organ; (ii) 'meddler' (i.e. he who has sexual intercourse); (pun, II i 36)
MEET, unite (III iii 120)
MEND, repair, improve (I Pr 14); 'God shall mend my soul', as I hope that God shall heal my soul, cure it from sin or fault
MERCY, 'cry you mercy', beg your pardon
MERIT BLISS, earn a place in heaven
MEW, shut up (in her room, as a hawk was enclosed in its 'mew' (= cage) while it was moulting)
MICKLE, great
MIDWIFE, i.e. she delivers men of their fancies by manifesting them in their dreams
MIND, opinion (IV i 4); thoughts (V ii 4); 'in mind', into the opinion that
MINDED, 'too much minded by herself alone', as her solitude allows her to brood upon it too much
MINE, of my opinion, persuaded by me (III v 192)
MINIM RESTS, *see under* RESTS
MINION, spoiled hussy
MINSTREL, a derogatory title for a musician, i.e. 'good-for-nothing'
MISADVENTUR'D, unfortunate
MISCHANCE BE SLAVE TO, one's passionate reaction to this misfortune be governed by
MISS, be inadequate (I Pr 14)
MIS-SHAPEN, badly-, evilly-formed (I i 177); ill-directed, with pun on 'shape' (III iii 131)
MISTEMPERED, (i) intemperately used; (ii) tempered (i.e., of a metal, repeatedly heated and doused in water to give it resilience and edge) with evil intent; (iii) tempered, i.e. (as in (ii)) 'cooled', not in water but in the blood of neighbours
MODERN, ordinary; 'Which modern lamentation might have moved', which (i.e. the news of her parents' death) might have provoked a common degree of sorrow (whereas news of Romeo's banishment necessarily provokes extraordinary anguish)
MOE, more
MOODY, irascible, angry; 'moody to be moved', angry at being provoked
MORROW, morning; 'Good morrow', (i) good morning (II iii 31); (ii) farewell (II iii 34)
MORTAL, deadly (V i 66)
MOST SOUGHT WHERE MOST MIGHT NOT BE FOUND, drove me to seek places where fewest people would be found
MOUSE-HUNT, a man who pursues women amorously by night (allusion to the proverb 'Cat after kind (i.e. after a mate) good mouse-hunt')
MOVE, (i) rouse to anger (I i 86); (ii) provoke (IV v 95); (iii) persuade (III iv 2, IV iii 4); (iv) may encourage (I iii 98); (v) make a movement; (vi) urge, take the initiative; (puns on (i), (ii), and (v), I i 5–10; (v) and (vi), I v 103–4)
MUCH, 'much to do with hate, but more with love', a great deal of turmoil connected with (in the street) enmity, (in me) love; 'much denied', (i) refused information vehemently and often; (ii) denied knowledge of a matter of great importance; 'much in years', many years older; 'much upon', close upon
MUFFLE, conceal (V iii 21)
MUFFLED, blindfolded (as Cupid was often depicted)
MUTINY, revolt, violent strife
MY HUSBAND IS ON EARTH . . . LEAVING EARTH, i.e. my husband is alive on this earth, and my holy marriage vow is registered in heaven; how, therefore, can I be absolved from my vow and thus be able to marry Paris, except by the death of my husband

NATIVE, (i) original, where you originated from (III ii 102); (ii) normal, natural (IV i 97)
NATURAL (adj.), kindly; (n.), congenital idiot
NAUGHT, wicked
NEAR, close to the target (I i 203); 'come near', struck home, hit upon the truth
NEEDLY, of necessity
NEIGHBOUR, neighbouring
NICE, trivial
NIMBLE-PINION'D, swift-winged (*see* DOVES)
NINE LIVES, allusion to the popular theory that cats have nine lives

NONE, 'she will none', she refuses to have anything to do with it; 'none ill', no bad ones
NONE BUT FOR SOME, none without some such good use
NOTE (v.), (i) notice (I v 69, V i 38); (ii) pay attention to; (iii) supply with musical notes; (iv) find fault with; (pun on (ii), (iii) and (iv), IV v 115ff)
NOTHING, in no way, not at all (I i 110); no wound at all (III i 89); 'I am nothing slow to slack his haste', I intend in no way at all to retard his hastiness by my own sluggardliness
NUMBERS, 'for the numbers', inclined to write metrical verse (in this case in the form of the Petrarchan love-sonnet)

O, exclamation of lamentation (III iii 90)
OBSEQUIES, funeral rites
OCCASION, (i) need, (ii) cause; 'take some occasion without giving', find an excuse without having to be given a cause
OCCUPY, (i) prolong, dwell upon; (ii) deal with sexually; (this was considered to be an indecent word)
ODD, 'and odd', and a few more
O'ERPERCH, fly over
OF, from (I v 141, I i 175)
OFF, whole, in one draught
OFFICE, 'leave it for my office', left instructions that it should be my duty to do so
OFFICER, officer of the town guard
OLD, inveterate, hardened (III iii 94)
ON, often = 'of'; 'on Romeo cries', cries out against Romeo
ON PART AND PART, some on one side and some on the other
ONE, ''Tis all one', it's all the same
OPE HER LAP, (i) spread her skirt to help her to catch; (ii) yield her chastity (allusion to the myth of Danaë, who was seduced by Jupiter in the guise of a shower of gold)
OPERATION, intoxicating influence
OPPRESSION, I iv 24, (i) (mental) affliction; (ii) (physical) pressure, burden (pun)
ORB, 'circled orb', the moon's sphere (*see* SPHERES)
ORDER, religious order (of St Francis)
ORISONS, prayers
ORNAMENTS, dress, attire, equipment
OSIER CAGE, basket made of willow-twigs
OUT, (i) expired (I iv 3); exclamation of indignation (III v 156); 'out upon', away with (expression of indignation); exclamation of woe, lamentation (IV v 25)
OUTRAGE, 'mouth of outrage', utterance of shocked sorrow
OVERWHELMING, overhanging
OWES, owns

PACK, knapsack
PALMER'S KISS, the kiss which pilgrims ('palmers') give (i.e. the touching of palms rather than of hands)
PALY, pale
PARAMOUR, lover, mistress
PARDON, 'I'll pardon you', I'll give you leave to go (i.e. I'll throw you out); 'pardon me's', i.e. Mercutio mocks the affected use of this phrase
PART, 'that part cheers each part', its smell restores the whole body (of him who smells it); 'Your part', i.e. Juliet's mortal body (IV v 69); 'his part', i.e. Juliet's soul (IV v 70)
PARTIES OF SUSPICION, suspected persons
PARTIZANS, spears with broad blades
PARTS, personal qualities, accomplishments, excellence
PASS, walk along (II iii 63)
PASSADO, lunging thrust
PASSAGE, course
PASS'D, excelled
PASTRY, part of kitchen where the pastry is made
PATH, 'day's path', the pathway daily traversed by the sun through the sky
PAY, 'pay the forfeit', *see* FORFEIT; 'pay that doctrine', supply that teaching (to pay Romeo back for the advice he has given him)
PEEVISH, obstinate, perverse
PENALTY, 'in penalty alike', under threat of the same punishment
PENCIL, paintbrush
PENNYWORTHS, i.e. full money's worth
PENS, confines
PEPPERED, finished, given my death blow
PERFORCE, forcibly, by force
PERILOUS, dangerous, horrible, awful
PETRARCH, Italian poet (1304–74) whose love-sonnets to the chaste Laura de Noves became a model for love-poetry, in particular for the tearful ('flow'd') celebration of the pangs of unfulfilled love
PHAETHON, son of Phoebus Apollo. He asked to drive his father's sun-chariot for a day, but, when his wish had been granted, he found himself too weak to guide the horses, and they bolted, causing the chariot to pass close enough to the earth to scorch its surface.

To prevent the earth from burning up, Zeus killed him with a thunderbolt

PHOEBUS, Apollo, the sun-god

PHYSIC, art of healing (in this the priest's role of performing the marriage-rite)

PILCHER, leather coat, i.e. scabbard

PIN, bull's eye, stud in the centre of the archer's target

PINK, (i) perfect example; (ii) a flower; (iii) ornamental perforation (puns, II iv 56ff)

PITCH, the height to which a falcon soars before descending upon its prey

PLANTAIN, 'Your plantain leaf', (it's common knowledge that) the leaf of the plantain (which was used to bind trivial wounds) can be used for that, i.e. Benvolio's advice underestimates the seriousness of Romeo's wound

PLEASURE, 'our further pleasure', what else I desire to be done; 'on their pleasure stay', lie entirely at their disposal

POIS'D, balanced, weighed

POOR-JOHN, 'thou had'st been poor-John', you would have been mere dried fish, i.e. no good as a woman (fish = prostitute)

POP'RIN PEAR, a type of pear which resembles a penis in shape

PORTENTOUS, of evil omen

PORTLY, dignified, well-mannered

POSSESS'D, (of a home) taken possession of, moved into; 'love itself possess'd', love possessed in reality

POST, 'took post', started out with post horses, i.e. as swiftly as I could, (the swiftest means of travelling overland was by using the post-horse system, which was so organised that fresh horses were stabled at inns at intervals along a route, so that no sooner had one horse become tired than it could be replaced by another fresh one); 'in post', hastily, by means of post horses

POST-HORSES, *see* POST

POTHECARY, apothecary, druggist

POWDER, gunpowder

POX, 'The pox of', a plague (usually syphilis) upon

PRACTICE STRATAGEMS, play devious tricks upon

PRATING, idly chattering

PREFIXED, prearranged

PRESENCE, demeanour (I v 71); 'feasting presence', large reception-room (in a great house) specially arranged for a feast

PRESENT, immediate (IV i 61); 'whose sale is present death', to sell which would incur the penalty of instant execution

PRESENTLY, immediately

PRESERVING, which prolongs life and stops decay (with allusion to the preservation of fruit by boiling it in sugar)

PREST, 'to have it prest With', if you increase the oppression by adding

PRICE, worth; 'the price of his dear blood doth owe', should pay the penalty for the murder of the dear Mercutio

PRICK (n.), (i) point (on a clock); (ii) penis; (v.), remove with a needle (I iv 66); 'Prick love with pricking', (i) cause love to smart in retaliation for its tormenting you; (ii) make love to your beloved for the pleasure of so doing; (pun)

PRICK-SONG, 'as you sing prick-song', as precisely and formally as one would sing from printed music (rather than by ear)

PRIDE, 'tis much pride', it is a fine thing

PRINCE OF CATS, allusion to the medieval story of Reynard the Fox, the cat in which is called Tibert or Tybalt

PRINCOX, insolent youngster

PRIVY, a partaker in the secret

PROCEEDING, the progress, course, of your feud

PROCURE, (i) arrange, persuade (II ii 145); (ii) bring (III v 67)

PRODIGIOUS, monstrous, deformed, ill-omened

PROFANE, soil, sully by treating in an unworthy way

PROFANERS OF THIS NEIGHBOUR-STAINED STEEL, you who misuse your swords by staining them with the blood of your neighbours

PROMISE, amuse

PROMOTION, social advancement

PROOF (adj.), invulnerable; (n.), tested or proved armour (I i 208); 'in proof', in practice, when actually experienced

PROPAGATE, augment

PROPERER, more handsome

PROPORTION, rhythm

PROROGUE, defer, postpone; 'death prorogued wanting of thy love', a delayed death lacking your love

PROSPEROUS, successful

PROTEST, make a formal declaration (of love) (II iv 171)

PROVERB'D WITH A GRANDSIRE PHRASE, equipped with an ancient and ven-

erable proverbial saying (allusion to the proverb, 'A good candle-holder proves a good gamester', *see* CANDLE-HOLDER)
PUFFS, (i) swells in anger; (ii) blows
PULING, whimpering
PUMP, low single-soled shoe
PUNTO REVERSO, back-handed thrust
PURBLIND, blind or dim-sighted
PURCHASE OUT, buy immunity from the punishment for
PURG'D, cleansed; 'Being purg'd', once it has been purified
PURPOSE, 'not to the purpose', of no importance
PURSUED MY HUMOUR, NOT PURSUING HIS, (i) indulged my inclination to solitude by not pursuing Romeo, who had similar feelings; (ii) followed my inclination for solitude by not demanding from Romeo the reason for his similar inclination
PUT OUT, display, prepare for use
PUT UP, sheathe; 'put up our pipes', (i) pack up our instruments; (ii) cease to speak, shut up
PUTTING ONE AWAY, discarding a third person (proverbial phrase implying that two people, but not three, can keep a secret)

QUEEN MAB, apparently Shakespeare's invention, perhaps a combination of 'quean' (= prostitute) and 'mab' (= slut)
QUESTION, 'call . . . in question more', summon . . . more into my thoughts
QUIT, requite (with payment)
QUOTE, observe

RAGE, insane fit, madness (IV iii 53)
RAISE A SPIRIT, conjure up a spirit (with innuendo, *see* CIRCLE) (II i 24)
RAIS'D, alerted
RANK, virulent, excessive, corrupt
RANK'D WITH, accompanied by
RAT-CATCHER, *see* PRINCE OF CATS
RATE (n.), 'at such rate be set', valued so highly; (v.), berate, reprove vehemently
RE, 'I'll re you, I'll fa you', names of the second and fourth notes in the musical scale, here used as comical verbs, i.e. I'll certainly thump you
REAR-WARD, rearguard (of a column of troops), i.e. subsequent or final event or blow (pun on 'rear-word')
REASON COLDLY OF, soberly discuss
REASON'S MERRIMENT, the source of joy to the calm intellect (which rejoices in the knowledge of spiritual salvation)
REBECK, three-stringed fiddle-like instrument
RECK'NING, calculation
RECKONING, reputation, public esteem
RECLAIM'D, brought back into obedience
REEKY SHANKS, shin-bones that give off foul vapours
REFLEX, reflection
REFUSE, abjure
RESIGN, 'to earth resign', submit to death
RESPECT, 'In one respect', because of one thing
RESPECTIVE LENITY, gentleness governed by discrimination or discretion
REST (n.), 'set up his rest', (in a card game) staked all that he has, i.e. is fully determined; 'set up my everlasting rest', establish my resting-place for eternity (with pun on 'stake my final bet'); (v.), grant rest to (I iii 19); 'rest you merry', may God keep you happy (i.e. Goodbye)
RESTORATIVE, beneficial medicinal drink
RESTS HIS MINIM RESTS . . . BOSOM, he carefully makes the correct short pauses, feinting (i.e. pretending to attack) once, twice, then landing his point upon your breast
RETORTS, returns
RIBAND, ribbon
ROAR'D IN, experienced and shrieked at in, i.e. worthy to be suffered only in
ROE, 'without his roe', (i) an emaciated good-for-nothing (like a female herring that has deposited all its eggs); (ii) without his female deer (i.e. 'dear' = love); (iii) (perhaps) a play on the sound of Romeo's name, and the similarity between 'meo' and 'O me', a cry of lamentation
ROOTETH, 'Westward rooteth from', grows to the west of
ROPERY, trickery, rascally talk
ROSEMARY, plant used as a symbol of remembrance at weddings and funerals, hence 'you and rosemary' implies that Juliet's 'sententious' (II iv 205) contains a pun on 'yew'
ROTE, 'did read by rote that could not spell', was like that of someone who could not even spell, pretending to read a book by reciting it from memory
RUDE, (i) violent (I iv 26); (ii) rough, coarse (I v 49); (iii) churlish (III iii 24)
RUN, pierced (as with a sword) (II iv 14)

RUNAGATE, runaway, vagabond
RUNAWAYS', (meaning obscure) perhaps (i) the sun's or Phaethon's horses (*see* PHAETHON); (ii) 'renegades' ', i.e. officious observers who would inform against Romeo and herself
RUSH'D ASIDE, forcibly overruled
RUSHES, reeds spread on the floor

SACK, plunder, pillage
SACRIFICES OF, atonement for
SADLY, soberly, seriously
SADNESS, 'in sadness', soberly, seriously (with pun on 'sorrow')
SAID, 'Well said', well done
SAINTS, the images of saints
SALE, 'whose sale is present death', to sell which would incur the penalty of instant death
SALLOW, sickly-yellow (i.e. with grief)
SAME, 'For all this same', in spite of all this
SCALES, set of scales (Romeo's eyes)
SCAPE, escape
SCATHE, harm, injure
SCOPE, area
SCORE, 'too much for a score', (i) too much for one to be expected to pay a score (= bill) for it; (ii) too much (i.e. repulsive) even for twenty people
SCURVY, contemptible
SEAL'D, legally joined (as legal documents are ratified by being given a seal) (IV i 56)
SEARCHERS, health officials (appointed to view bodies and ascertain cause of death)
SEASON, (i) preserve (by salting); (ii) give flavour to
SECRET, discreet, reticent (II iv 190)
SENSE, (i) meaning (I i 26); (ii) 'take it in sense', feel it; (pun on (i) and (ii), I i 26–7)
SENSELESS, (i) incapable of feeling or perception; (ii) stupid, silly
SENTENCE, maxim
SENTENTIOUS, malapropism for 'sentence' = witty saying
SERVING-CREATURE, a derogatory term, i.e. 'mere lackey'
SETTLED, congealed
SEVERING, (i) broken apart (by the 'streaks'); (ii) causing the lovers to separate
SHADOWS, 'but love's shadows', mere dreams of love (V i 11)
SHAFT, arrow
SHAKE, QUOTH THE DOVE-HOUSE, i.e. 'the dove-cot trembled'
SHAME, an affront which shall shame us (I v 80); disgrace (IV i 74)
SHARPS, shrill high-pitched notes
SHIRT AND A SMOCK, man and a woman
SHRIFT, absolution; 'to hear true shrift', as to hear a truthful confession (from Romeo)
SHRINE, i.e. Juliet's hand
SHRIV'D, absolved
SIMPLE, foolish; plain, mere (III 2 16)
SIMPLENESS, folly, stupidity
SINGLENESS, (i) fact of being unique; (ii) simplicity, silliness
SINGLE-SOL'D, (i) (of a pump) having only one sole; (ii) thin, weak (of a jest)
SINK IN IT, (i) be oppressed by it; (ii) have sexual intercourse
SIR-REVERENCE, if you'll pardon the disrespect (a mock apology)
SIRRAH, term of address, contempt, reprimand, or implying an assumption of authority on the part of the speaker
SKAINS-MATES, perhaps (i) 'skenes-mates' = dagger-companions, i.e. ruffians; (ii) 'skeins-mates' = 'yarn-companions', 'sempstresses', i.e. loose women
SLACK, *see* NOTHING
SLAVE, servile, obsequious fellow (I i 13)
SLAYS ALL SENSES WITH THE HEART, kills the heart, and (therefore) the whole body
SLEEP IN QUIET, (i) be dead; (ii) sleep peacefully in my arms (Juliet's secret ambiguity)
SLIP, (i) evasive action; (ii) counterfeit coin; (pun)
SLOP, 'French slop', short loose-hanging breeches
SLUG-A-BED, tardy-riser
SMATTER, go chatter
SMOOTH, speak kindly
SO, as (I ii 3); if only, provided that, in order that (II ii 97)
SO HO!, hunter's cry on sighting the quarry, i.e. 'I've seen through you!'
SO PLEASE YOU, please be so good as to (I i 154); if you please (IV iii 9)
SOCIETY, the presence of other people
SOFT, 'but soft', wait!
SOLELY SINGULAR, absolutely unripe, unmatched
SOLEMN, appropriate to ceremony (here, to a wedding)
SOLEMNITY, ceremony
SOME, a mere (V iii 256)
SOON-SPEEDING GEAR, a substance of rapid operation

SORT, choose
SOUND (v.), III ii 126, (i) express; (ii) fathom, measure the depth of; make music (IV v 131)
SOUNDING, being open to the measuring of his depth, investigation of his innermost feelings by others (I i 148); 'for sounding', as payment, or to clink together (IV v 137)
SOUNDLY, thoroughly; (pun on 'with musical sounds', IV v 109)
SOUNDPOST, the piece of wood which supports the belly of a violin or similar instrument, and connects the belly and the back
SPANISH BLADES, allusion to the fact that the Spaniards (especially those of Toledo) were renowned for the high quality of the sword-blades which they made
SPARE NOT FOR COST, don't stint yourself through fear of excessive expenditure
SPARING, (i) economy, thrift; (ii) refraining
SPED, dispatched, done for
SPEED, 'be my speed', grant me swiftness
SPENT, (i) used up (II iv 129); (ii) shed, expended (III ii 130)
SPHERES, (i) allusion to the system of transparent concentric spheres upon which, according to the contemporary pre-Copernican cosmology, the heavenly bodies were placed, so as to revolve around the earth; (ii) eye-sockets
SPINNERS', spiders'
SPIT, transfix, impale
SPITE, (i) contemptuous defiance, malice, hatred (I i 77, I v 62); (ii) malicious injury (IV i 31); 'in spite of me', to scorn me; 'some spite', a very malicious, hateful thing
SPLEEN, irascibility, impetuosity
STALE, (i) (adj.) old, gone off; (ii) (n.) prostitute; (pun)
STAND (n.), coming to rest; (v.), not retreat, stand one's ground (with innuendo) (I i 20); insist (II iv 32); 'mine, being one, may stand in number, though in reck'ning none', (i) my daughter, though insignificant, being but one among many, may yet serve to swell the total (of fair women present); (ii) my daughter, there being only one of her, may take her place in the calculation of the number present, although the figure '1' is not itself considered to be a number (allusion to the proverb, 'One is as good as none'); 'stand to', maintain, acknowledge (II iv 140)
STAR-CROSSED, destined by the stars to be thwarted
STARK, rigid, incapable of movement
STARS, III ii 22, allusion to the classical notion that the illustrious dead are transformed into stars; the embodiment of astrological influence, of fortune (V i 24, V iii 111); planets (II ii 15)
STATE, (i) pomp (I iv 70); (ii) condition (IV iii 4); (iii) (high) rank, status (III iii 34); (iv) predicament (III iii 166); (v) dignity, ceremony (IV iii 8)
STAY, wait; stop; endure (I i 210); wait for (III v 142); delay (V iii 250); 'on their pleasure stay', lie entirely at their disposal
STEADS, benefits
STEEDS, 'fiery-footed steeds', the horses which draw the chariot of the sun-god Phoebus Apollo through the sky to his night's resting-place in the west
STEEL, swords (I i 80)
STILL, always
STOCK, family, ancestry; 'stock and honour', honourable stock
STONE, testicle
STORE, accumulated and abundant treasure; (valuable) number (I ii 22); 'with beauty dies her store', when she dies, all she dies possessed of will be beauty
STRAIN, pervert, force awry
STRANGE, (i) belonging to a stranger (i.e. someone other than Romeo) (II i 25); (ii) distant, reserved (II ii 101); (iii) unfamiliar, (hence) shy (III ii 15)
STRANGER IN, unaccustomed to
STRANGLED, suffocated
STRATAGEMS, plots, tricks
STUMBLING ON ABUSE, (i) if by chance abused; (ii) turning awkwardly towards corruption; (iii) being corrupted by misuse
SUBTLY, deceitfully, treacherously, cunningly
SUIT, (i) request (I ii 6); (ii) a petition, often from a private individual to a member of the nobility, by the handling of which as an intermediary the courtier could hope to earn a fee (I iv 78); (iii) wooing, courtship; (both (i) and (iii), II ii 152)
SULLEN, mournful (IV v 88)
SUM UP SUM, calculate even the total of
SUPPLE GOVERNMENT, the power of ready and nimble movement
SUPPOS'D, 'foe supposed', she who is believed (by others) to be his enemy
SURCEASE, cease
SURE WIT, accurate, infallible power of humorous invention
SWASHING, slashing, forceful

SWEET (adv.), kindly (II ii 72); sweetly (II iii 32); (n.) sweet drink or fragrance (I i 192); sweetness, delight (II Pr 14)

SWEETING, sweet apple

SWITS AND SPURS), (urge your horse of wit to a gallop with) switches (= thin riding whips or branches) and spurs

SWOUNDED, swooned

SYMPATHY, 'woeful sympathy', agreement in feeling woe

TACKLED STAIR, rope ladder

TAKE, 'take him down', humble him, rebuke him; 'take me with you', explain this clearly to me, so that I can understand; 'take our good meaning . . . wits', don't be so literal, but understand the true meaning of what I say, for the true discretion in my underlying meaning is five times as significant as that expressed in my actual words; 'take the law of our sides', keep on the right side of the law; 'take the wall of', walk at the side of the road by the wall (i.e. in the best and cleanest part of the street), at the expense of; 'take truce', make a truce, effect a reconciliation; 'take you in your bed', find you still in bed (with innuendo)

TALE, II iv 91–92, (i) story, (ii) 'tail' (i.e. penis)

TALK'D ON, 'they are not to be talk'd on', they are not worth talking about

TALL, valiant

TALLOW-FACE, pallid waxen-face

TARTAR'S PAINTED BOW OF LATH, a lip-shaped bow of Tartar design (the traditional shape of Cupid's bow) made out of a thin piece of painted wood

TASSEL-GENTLE, i.e. 'tercel-gentle', the male falcon

TEAT, 'thy teat', the nipple (the Nurse's own) that you sucked

TEEN, sorrow

TELL, count, reckon (I ii 12)

TEMPER (n.), (i) mental disposition; (ii) quality of hardness and elasticity imparted to steel during manufacture; (v.), (i) mix, compound; (ii) modify, moderate (its evil potency)

TEMPER'D, blended, balanced

TEMP'RING, mollifying, moderating, blending

TEMPT, test, make trial of, try to make him contradict himself

TENDER (n.), offer (III iv 12); 'in her fortune's tender', at the very moment when her luck offers her an excellent opportunity (for marriage); (v.), value

TERMS, (rhetorical) phrases

TETCHY, fretful, peevish

TEXT, 'a certain text', a very true maxim

THEREWITHAL, with it (i.e. the poison)

THIEVISH WAYS, roads made dangerous by robbers

THISBE, the beloved of Pyramus. According to Ovid, both committed suicide for love, each mistakenly thinking the other to be dead

THOU'S, thou shalt, you must (I iii 10)

THRILLS, that induces shivers

THRIVE, 'so thrive my soul', as my immortal soul may be saved from damnation

THRUST TO THE WALL, i.e. in amorous assault

TIDE, time, season

TILTS, thrusts

TIME, 'keeps time, distance, and proportion', carefully regulates his fencing movements, his distance from his opponent, and the rhythm of his movements; 'In good time', just in time

TIMELESS, untimely

TITAN'S FIERY WHEELS, the wheels of the sun-god Hyperion, who was one of the Titans (the gods who, in classical myth, existed before the gods of Olympus), and who rode through the sky on a fiery chariot

TITHE-PIG'S, a pig given to the local parson by his parishioners in payment of the 'tithe' (a tax of one tenth of the year's produce levied to support the Church)

TO, go to (I ii 44); in order to (II ii 173); compared to (II iv 39); 'all the world to nothing', I would bet the whole world against nothing

TO DO, turmoil

TO-NIGHT, last night

TOOK, interpreted (II iv 121)

TOOL, sword

TOPGALLANT, highest platform or sail on a ship

TOWARDS, in preparation, about to take place (I v 120)

TOY, whim

TRACES, harness

TRAFFIC, business (two hours seems to have been the usual duration of an Elizabethan play)

TRANSPARENT, (i) translucent; (ii) easily detected; (pun)

TRENCHER, wooden dish
TRESPASS, transgression, sin
TRIBUTARY, paying tribute
TRICK, quirk of behaviour, capricious behaviour
TRIED, tested and been proven to be
TRIM, cleanly, accurately, neatly (allusion to a line of the ballad of King Cophetua which describes Cupid 'that shoots so trim')
TRIUMPHANT, glorious
TROW, 'I trow', (i) I'm sure; (ii) (expletive) I suppose (II v 62)
TRUCE, 'take truce', make a truce, effect a reconciliation
TRUCKLE BED, low bed on wheels which can be stored beneath another more permanent bed
TRUDGE, 'to bid me trudge', for someone to ask me to be off
TRUMPET, allusion to the 'last trump' of I Corinthians xv 52, the trumpet that would sound to signal the destruction of the world before the Second Coming of Christ
TRUNK, body
TRY, (i) find out (IV ii 3); (ii) test (IV ii 5)
TUNERS OF ACCENT, meddlers with speech-habits
TUTOR ME FROM, instruct me to avoid
TWAIN, 'shall be twain', shall be separated, at enmity

UMPIRE, legal arbitrator (a legal third party whose job it was to decide a matter disputed between two otherwise irreconcilable persons or factions)
UNACCUSTOMED, unusual, unfamiliar (i.e. poisonous)
UNATTAINTED, free from blemish, unprejudiced
UNBOUND, (i) (of a book) incomplete, with loose leaves not yet bound together; (ii) yet unbound by the ties of marriage
UNBRUISED, unhurt (by care)
UNCOMFORTABLE, bringing discomfort, depriving us of comfort
UNEVEN IS THE COURSE, this manner of proceeding is irregular and fraught with difficulties
UNFURNISH'D, without proper preparations and provisions
UNHALLOWED, impious, sacrilegious
UNKIND, unnatural
UNKNOWN, 'Too early seen, and known too late', I saw him too soon, before I knew who he was, but now I do know his identity, it is too late (for I already love him)
UNLOOK'D FOR, unexpected
UNMANNED, (i) (of a hawk) undomesticated, unused to the presence of man, untrained; (ii) still virgin, chaste
UNSTUFF'D, not clogged with anxieties
UNTAUGHT, uneducated (i.e. ill-mannered) person
UNTHRIFTY, unfortunate, unlucky
UP, roused, in arms (III i 130)
URG'D, (i) mentioned; (ii) suggested (I v 107)
USE (n.), 'for use', to be used in or associated with ordinary life (I v 45); 'that fair use', proper beneficial function; (v.), (i) are accustomed (II Pr 10); (ii) have sexual intercourse with (II iv 147); (iii) behave towards (III i 76); (iv) lend out at interest (III iii 124)
UTTERS, sells, supplies

VALIDITY, value, worth
VANISH'D, was breathed from
VANITY, (i) frivolity (I i 176); (ii) worldly delight (II vi 20)
VAST, (i) extensive; (ii) desolate
VAULTY, arched, vaulted, domed
VENGE, avenge
VENUS, goddess of love
VERSAL, i.e. universal, whole
VESTAL, chaste
VIEW, (i) appearance (I i 167); (ii) eyesight (I i 169); (iii) viewing, inspection (I ii 32)
VILLAIN, base-minded low-born rustic, scoundrel
VISOR, (i) mask (I v 20); (ii) a face that is already as ugly as a mask; (both (i) and (ii), I iv 30)

WALK, i.e. come with me to fight (III i 73)
WANT, lack, need; 'to want thy light', lacking the light of your presence
WANTING THAT, lacking that, if I am unable to do that
WANTON (adj.), uncontrollable (II v 70); sportive, frolicsome (II vi 19); (n.), unrestrained merry-maker (I iv 35); a spoiled, capricious child (II ii 178)
WARD, youth under guardianship, i.e. below 21 years of age
WARE, (i) aware; (ii) careful to avoid
WARNS, summons
WARRANT, 'I warrant', I guarantee
WATCH (n.), night-guard, watchmen (III iii 148); 'keep his watch', keeps his vigil, remains

awake; (v.), (i) vigilantly and protectively await (IV i 116); (ii) remain awake (IV iv 9); (iii) prevent with vigilance (with pun on (ii), IV iv 12)

WATCHING, remaining awake

WATER, 'sweet water', perfume

WAX, 'of wax', as perfect as a model, piece of sculpture

WAXES, grows

WAYS, 'go thy ways', go on your way

WEAKER VESSELS, metaphor for 'women', used in I Peter iii 7

WEAL, happiness

WEEDS, clothes (V i 39)

WELL-A-DAY, alas

WHAT, what useful purpose (I i 233); that which (II iii 10); 'What a', what kind of (II iv 110)

WHAT, HO, Hey! (shout to attract attention) (I i 81)

WHERE, place (I i 196)

WHEREFORE, why

WHIT, jot, little bit

WHITE-UPTURNED, directed towards the sky so the ordinary onlooker on the same plane can only see their whites

WHO, him who (I i 128)

WHORESON, fellow (literally 'bastard')

WILD-GOOSE CHASE, cross-country horse-race, in which each successive horse has to follow at an interval the exact path of the leader (like a flight of wild geese)

WILL, what he desires (I i 170); wish (I iii 7); 'my will to her consent is but a part', my own desire is nothing without her consent; 'rude will', the coarse capacity to respond to fleshly desire

WINDOWS, shutters; 'eye's windows', i.e. eyelids

WINK, shut, i.e. connive at, overlook (III ii 6); 'winking at', overlooking

WINNING, 'lose a winning match', lose (i.e. her virginity) and yet at the same time win a competition (i.e. gain a husband)

WISELY TOO FAIR, too prudently virtuous

WITH, 'Was I with you there for the goose?', did I manage to keep up with you and prove you a simpleton?

WIT, (i) understanding, intelligence; (ii) wisdom (III v 73); 'no wit', unwise

WITHAL, by this (I i 110); with (I v 113); in addition (III i 151)

WITHOUT, outside (III iii 17); 'without a sudden calm', unless there occurs a sudden and immediate lull in the storm; 'without book', (i) by heart (I ii 59); (ii) memorised (I iv 7)

WITS, 'five wits', the sum total of my wisdom

WOE, 'that name's woe', the anguish caused by (the mention of) that name

WOLVISH-RAVENING LAMB, lamb which is as carnivorously predatory as a wolf (allusion to Matthew vii 15, 'Beware of false prophets, which come to you in sheep's clothing, but inwardly they are ravening wolves')

WOMB, belly

WORLD'S EXILE, banishment from the world

WORM PRICK'D FROM, worm removed with a pin from (allusion to the popular belief that worms bred within the fingers of idle maidens)

WORMWOOD, (the juice of) a plant of proverbially bitter taste

WOT, know

WOULD, 'I would thou wert so happy by thy stay', I wish you would be so fortunate in your visit

WOUNDED, i.e. with one of Cupid's arrows (II iii 50)

WREAK, (i) avenge; (ii) give expression to

WRENCHING IRON, a form of crowbar

WRETCH, term of endearment (I iii 45); 'worthless miserable creature' (III v 160)

WRITTEN, 'It is written', allusion to a passage in Lyly's *Euphues* of which this passage of Shakespeare's is a parody

YARD, a tailor's yard-measure (with innuendo)

YEAR, 'at twelve year old', when I was twelve

YOND, yonder

YOUR, I ii 51, used to introduce a phrase that is common knowledge or a cliché, i.e. 'It is said that, it is common knowledge that'

ZOUNDS, By God's wounds (sustained when on the Cross)